From The Age
Of Gi

Alfred the Great

MOGZILLA

Chester

NORTH WALES

Shrewsbury

Wedne

Buttington

M

Bridgenorth

Magesæt

Worc

Brecknock

Hereford

Dyfed

Gwent

R. Sev

Caerleon

Morganwg

Pucklechurch

Bristol

Bath

Wedmore

Wells

Watchet

Aller

Glaston

Athelney

Somerton

Appledore

Taunton

Sherborn

W E

Axminster

Dorchester

EXETER

Corfes

Gafulford

WEST WALES

Hengestesdun

Gainas
Lindesey
kland
Nottingham
R. Trent
Repton
Holland
Crowland
Medeshampsted
(Peterborough)
Tamworth
E R C I A
hall
Northfolk
Norwich
EAST
ANGLIA
Southfolk
R. Nen
R. Ouse
Warwick
Bedford
Burford
Kirtlington
Cirencester
Hertford
Essex
Bensington
St. Albans
Cricklade
Wallingford
M.sex
LONDON
Wantage
R. Thames
Wanborough
I. Sheppey
Æscesdun
Reading
Merton
Basing
X
Surrey
CANTERBURY
E
Ockley
Kent
WINCHESTER
Andredesweald
Appledore
Salisbury
Sussex
Wimborne
Swanwick

Key Events that occurred before the events in this book

840 – Aethelwulf becomes King of Wessex

849 – Alfred born in Wantage

849 – Aethelwulf and Aethelbald defeat Vikings at Aclea

855 - Vikings settle on the Isle of Sheppey

855 – Alfred travels to Rome with his father Aethelwulf

855 - Aethelbald rules West Wessex in absence of the king

856 – King Aethelwulf marries Judith and returns to Wessex

856 – Aethelbald refuses to return West Wessex (Winchester) to his father

856 – Aethelbehrt allows his father, King Aethelwulf, to rule East Wessex

858 – King Aethelwulf dies. Aethelbehrt reclaims East Wessex

858 – Aethelbald marries his father's widow and his own stepmother - Judith

Key Events that occurred after the events in this book

861– Alfred learns to read and write

865 – Aethelbehrt dies. Aethelred rules Wessex.

865 – Great Viking army invades led by the sons of Ragnar.

871 – Vikings attack Wessex. Aethelred dies after the Battle of Merton.

871 – Alfred crowned King of Wessex

877/878 – Alfred flees the Viking army and hides in the marshes

878 – Alfred victorious in the Battle of Edington defeating Guthrum's army

886 – Alfred and Guthrum agree to divide Mercia between them

899 – Alfred the Great dies. His son Edward the Elder is King of Wessex.

Anglo-Saxons in 858 AD

It was the custom in the Anglo-Saxon period for all members of a noble family to have names beginning with the same letter. Alfred's family took this one step further: he was the only child of King Aethelwulf to not begin with the word 'Aethel' – meaning noble. Ironically, he was to become the most noble member of his family.

The Royal Family

Alfred (8*) – Youngest son of King Aethelwulf and Queen Osburh. Couldn't read or write.

Aethelbald (26*) – Alfred's oldest brother. King of West Wessex. Rules from Winchester. Married to Judith. A determined fighter.

Aethelbehrt (24*) – Alfred's brother. King of East Wessex. Rules from Canterbury. Mild-mannered and monastic. Friendly with the Viking Sigurd.

Aethelswith (16*) – Alfred's sister. Married to Burgred – king of Mercia.

Aethelred (13*) – Alfred's youngest brother and friend. Prefers praying to fighting.

Judith (15*) – Daughter of French King Charles the Bald. Great Granddaughter of Emperor Charlemagne. Previously married to King Aethelwulf. Now married to King Aethelbald. Part-time tutor to Alfred.

**Approximate ages as exact dates of birth are not certain.*

Other Important People

Bishop Swithun (58*) – Tutor and friend of King Aethelwulf. Bishop of Winchester. Opposed to Aethelbald's marriage to Judith. Revered by the people of Winchester for his kindness.

Bishop Eahlstan – A Bishop for over 50 years. A famous fighter and Viking hater. Friend to King Aethelbald and a Councillor of War.

Weland – a Viking mercenary who fights anyone for enough money – including other Vikings.

Fictional Characters

Jarl Sigurd (52) – Viking war chief. King Aethelbehrt has given him lands and in return he has vowed to fight any other Viking invaders.

Godric (17) – Monk and Alfred's scribe. A skilled healer.

Wilfred (9) – A headstrong and angry boy. Sent to a monastery from a young age.

Mildryd (9) – A feisty young female who wants to become a warrior. Alfred's friend.

Osric (36)– A formidable fighter who trains the noble boys to become fighters.

Wulfric and Wulfstan (13) – Terrible teenage twins and sons of Osric. They hate Alfred and Aethelred.

Magen (38) – fighting monk and friend of Alfred.

Hacker (46) – Famed warrior with a blood-stained beard.

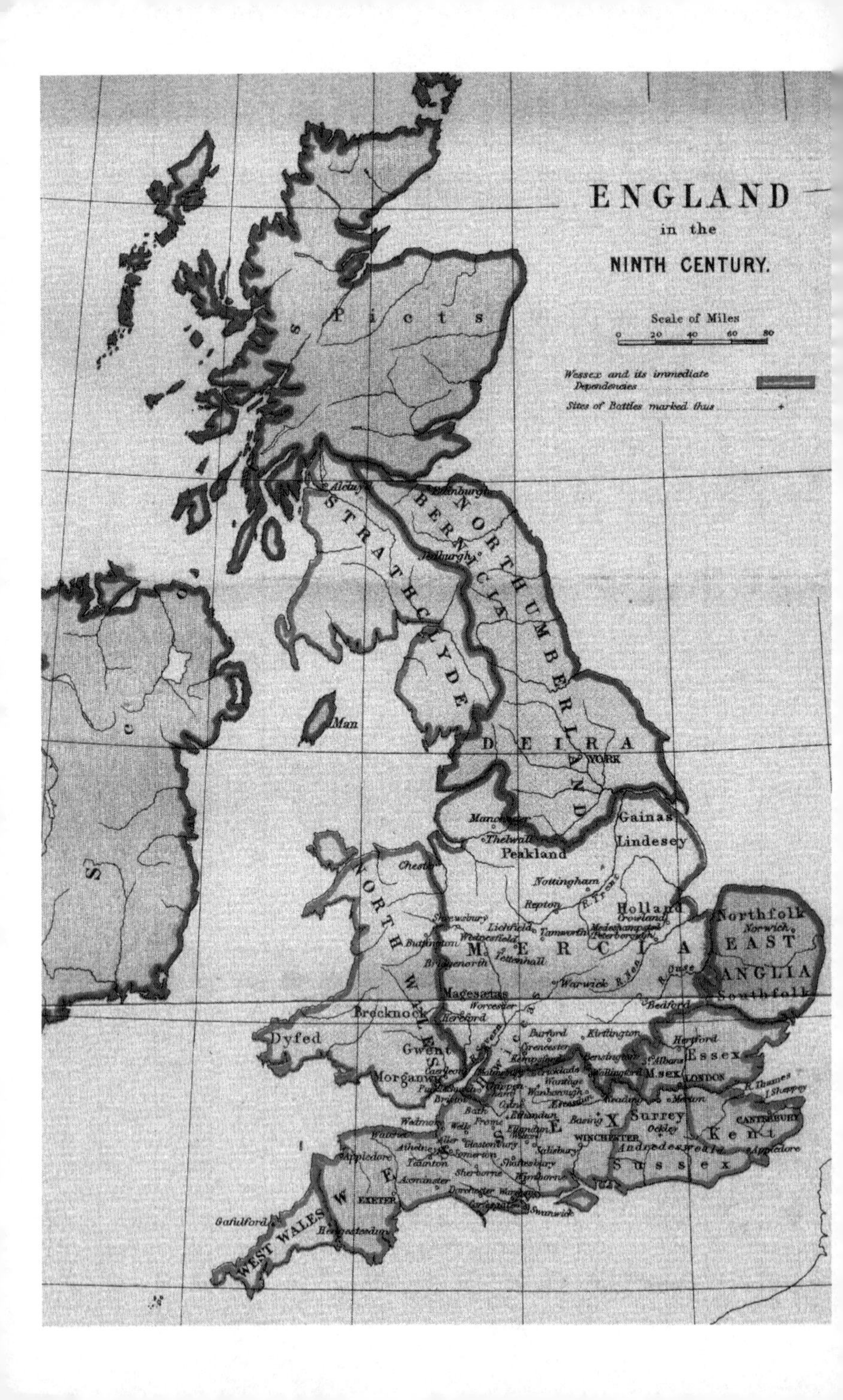
ENGLAND
in the
NINTH CENTURY.
Scale of Miles
0 20 40 60 80
Wessex and its immediate Dependencies
Sites of Battles marked thus +
Picts
STRATHCLYDE
BERNICIA
NORTHUMBERLAND
DEIRA
YORK
Man
Gainas
Lindesey
Peakland
Holland
Northfolk
Norwich
EAST ANGLIA
Southfolk
MERCIA
Nottingham
Repton
Lichfield
Tamworth
Chester
NORTH WALES
Dyfed
Brecknock
Gwent
Morganwg
Bedford
Essex
LONDON
Surrey
Kent
CANTERBURY
Sussex
WINCHESTER
WESSEX
EXETER
WEST WALES
Swanwick
Bath
Bristol
Frome
Glastonbury
Sherborne
Shaftesbury
Wimborne
Taunton
Axminster
Athelney
Appledore
Warwick
Worcester
Hereford
Magesætas
Bridgenorth
Tettenhall
Wednesfield
Buttington
Mancunium
Thelwall
Edinburgh
Jedburgh
Alclwyd

Prologue

Much is known of Alfred the Great – the wise, noble king who famously defeated the Viking army at Edington and finally brought peace to Wessex. However, far less is know about Alfred the boy, with very little recorded during the dates covered in this book. Perhaps this is because so little was expected of the frail and youngest member of his family.

It was a period of fear and fighting – with the threat of Viking attacks ever present and noble families doing whatever it took to grab power for themselves. Undoubtedly, Alfred would have had to grow up very quickly – with little time for a childhood.

What follows, is the result of detailed research, threading real-life events, such as the Viking attack on Winchester in 860AD and the death of his brother, King Aethelbald, with what we know of Alfred – the man.

The story shows how Alfred was influenced by these events and by the people known to be close to him, such as Bishop Swithun. Using these people, along with some fictional characters, a story unfolds that explains just how Alfred the boy, began his journey to greatness.

Paperback edition: ISBN: 9781914426025
Text copyright Paul Nolan
Cover by Rebecca Davy.
Cover ©Mogzilla 2020
Printed in the UK.
First published by Mogzilla in 2021.

Author's acknowledgement:

The author would like to thank the following people: Mum and Dad, Jake, Harry, Miranda and Robin.

858 AD
Winchester
August 17th

"One day Alfred, you are going to be great, so great that you must write about your life. People will want to know about one of the greatest men ever to have lived."
I thought this was one of Bishop Swithun's jokes, so I waited for a smile that never came.
"I know what you're thinking," he said. "How can the youngest of four princes ever become great?"
I nodded my head and smiled even though I was thinking of something completely different.
"A man isn't judged by where his life begins but by where it ends Alfred. And I know that true greatness awaits you. I have seen in you the same wisdom that your father had, but unlike him, you have the courage to make good use of it."
The bishop spoke with such kindness that I almost believed him. He is the wisest man I know, but how wise can a man be if he thinks an eight-year-old boy who doesn't know his letters can write about his life?
The bishop stepped to his left, revealing a much shorter, thinner and younger man.
"This is Godric," the bishop announced, "he will be your scribe. The words in your diary will come from your mouth but flow from Godric's quill. Trust him as you would trust me Alfred."
Like the bishop, Godric was a man of God. He was dressed in a brown tunic, with a plain cross at his neck.

Godric was staring, not at me, but at the huge Viking banner which hung beside my bed. He was obviously dying to know where the heathen banner had come from. Only when the bishop called his name, did he manage to drag his eyes away from it.

"Godric has something for you," the bishop said. The young monk pulled out a parcel wrapped in cloth. I took it from him and opened it.

"A book!" I exclaimed, turning to the first page. Glowing softly, in the top left corner, was the most amazing thing I had ever seen: a large, beautiful letter B, painted with swirls of ruby red, lined by thick gold ink. Showers of painted angels stood singing within the letter.

"The treasure is not in the gold letters but in the words Alfred," the old bishop whispered. "In this book, you will find prayers and psalms. May these words bring you strength when you most need it."

I flicked through the book and was delighted to see that each page began as the first one did, with a beautifully illuminated golden letter in the top left corner. I stopped turning the pages when I reached the middle of the book.

"Godric's finest work," the bishop said softly. A large oak tree rose from the bottom of the book, its golden branches stretching to the far ends of the page, dipping to touch the small words beneath. I picked up my aestel and pointed its golden tip to a word.

"Your family tree," the bishop said. "Godric has worked night and day since the king's wedding to complete it."

The old bishop hunched over the book and spoke with an icy chill. "Your family tree has noble roots but has become gnarled and twisted. Your father has left behind many branches. But branches can grow in different shapes and directions. You must grow tall, towards the heavens, and be straight and strong for your people because there will be others who will try and bend and break you."

Bishop Swithun pulled me to one side, leaving Godric to wander closer to the Raven banner and the black and yellow Viking shields either side of it. "I have told Godric to write everything you tell him. No one else is to know about this diary Alfred; should it fall into the wrong hands it could be your undoing."

I was relieved when the warmth returned to the bishop's voice. "I'm sure that you and 'Godric the Unsteady' will get on very well as you have so much in common."

The small, shaven-headed monk in the brown, tatty tunic was still gazing up at the banner. "Yes, we could be brothers," I said to the bishop. We laughed together.

"Why 'Godric the Unsteady'?" I whispered. The bishop stopped smiling: "Let's hope you never have to find out."

August 20th

'Godric the Unspoken' would suit the monk much better as he is far happier writing words than speaking them. I can have a better conversation with my horse than I can with him. I may have upset him when I told him we don't have time to start every diary entry with a huge, illustrated, golden letter. Perhaps he doesn't like writing about himself or maybe he isn't happy that I keep asking about his nickname. I suppose I shouldn't upset my 'third-hand' as he could, after all, write anything he likes about me and I wouldn't know.

The only matter Godric is happy discussing is the diary. He is keen to take down as much detail as possible. For example, I'm tutored by my stepmother, Judith who is only fifteen. She's married to my brother Aethelbald – the king. That's right – my brother married my father's wife – soon after my father died in January. Like most of the witan, (the king's councillors) Bishop Swithun was against the marriage but was the only one brave enough to say so. When people speak against the king, they don't often speak again.

Judith met Godric for the first time today. My two teachers couldn't be more different: one is dressed in the finest red silk, sleeves embroidered with gold thread; the other is dressed in rough wool, his sleeves stained with blue ink. One is the silky-haired daughter of a foreign king, brought up in the magnificent Palace of Charlemagne. The other is the shaven-headed son of a pig-farmer.

Judith was not impressed by Godric and she insisted that he has to leave the room whenever she comes to teach me. She says that she cannot recount heroic tales of her Great-Grandfather Charlemagne, with the smell of onions around her. She has a point. The smell is so strong that Godric cannot take it all with him. It was late at night when Bishop Swithun walked into my room, carrying a large cloaked object and wearing a wide smile. The smile went when he saw Judith sat in the corner. There was an uneasy silence as the bishop waited for Judith to leave. She didn't move. Like me, she wanted to know what was beneath the cloak.

"I have brought you a new companion," the bishop said. "Someone who may well prove useful in times to come." The bishop lifted the black veil to reveal a cage. I stared into it: there was something moving inside. He moved the cage into the candlelight: a magnificent hawk was perched on a wooden pole, light twinkling upon its shiny, dappled feathers, its huge amber eyes fixed on me.

"He's gorgeous," I gushed. "Thank you, Bishop."

"She's gorgeous," the bishop corrected. "But beware Alfred, such beauty can hide danger."

The bishop pulled a piece of meat from beneath his cloak and tossed it into the cage. In the time it took me to blink, the hawk had ripped the meat to threads. Godric went white. Bishop Swithun bowed his head, smiled and left the room. Judith chased after him. Their conversation faded down the steps.

August 21st

Godric doesn't like Hilda because he says Hilda doesn't like Godric. He says Hilda spent much of the night sharpening her claws on the steel cage making a sound like a sword on a grinding wheel.

Godric worked through the night writing the diary and flattening more pages. He must also have mixed more ink as the room now smells of egg, as well as onion. How can it be that the son of pig-farmer can read and write but the son of a king can't? Bishop Swithun has promised that one day he will teach me my letters. All the best teachers, he says, are in Northumberland. I might bring this up when I dine with my brother – the king – tonight. It all depends on what sort of mood Aethelbald is in.

I didn't bring it up. Osric, one of my brother's most loyal and fearsome thanes, joined the family for dinner, and like the king, he favours the sword over the feather. He sat at the far end of the long oak table, helping himself to a variety of meats, fish and cheeses, with Judith, Aethelred and myself between him and the king.

Aethelbald has wasted no time decorating the walls of the Great Hall with his war and hunting trophies:

captured Viking banners and shields are evenly spaced out and below them hang an array of hideous animal skulls, each illuminated from beneath by a bright candle. Tonight, each time the light flickered, their shadows seemed to leap out towards us. Now taking pride of place at the far end of the hall is the vast Viking sail which Aethelbald helped capture. It seemed to sail again as its red and white stripes rippled gently above the crackling log fire.

Heroic deeds flowed quickly from the two warriors, as did the beer from their glass jars; the cupbearer constantly scurrying from one end of the table to the other. I think the two men would have exchanged past glories long into the night if it hadn't been for Judith's timely interruption.

"Forgive me," she began, speaking in French to hide her words from Osric, "but are we not here to discuss two warriors of the future, and not of the past?"

Aethelbald slammed his glass down and pointed his knife towards his bride. The glare she returned was every bit as sharp as the knife. The king slowly lowered the blade and then spoke calmly to his wife.

"Indeed. Indeed. My brothers: forgive two old fools reliving their glory days," he said, now facing Aethelred and myself. "I have invited Osric here as he will be overseeing your training. I'm sure that very soon you will be adding to our trophy collection," he added, pointing to the few spaces left on the wall.

"Not if my two boys beat you to it," Osric boomed. "Wulfric and Wulfstan are looking forward to fighting your two brothers," he roared. Without taking his eyes off me, he picked up a cooked lobster and ripped it in half.

I am closer in age and manner to Aethelred, than to my other brothers. He is only five years older and like me, isn't happy about becoming a warrior.

"Father promised me a life of prayer, not a life of blood," he mumbled, as we sat in a dark corner of my room.

"That promise died when father did," I reminded him. "What is it Aethelbald says? It will be steel not words that defeat the Danes."

Aethelred looked glumly at my mother's portrait:

"She wouldn't stand for this. Mother said we wouldn't have to follow our brothers into battle. She wanted more for us."

Bishop Swithun and Aethelred agree on this. The picture they paint of my mother is that of the kindest and most holy of women, whose love of God was almost equal to the love she had for her children. She died when I was only four, so this is how I see her too.

Aethelred wished me goodnight when Godric entered the room. I knew the Prince of Wessex would love to swap places with the shabbily dressed monk. Being born into the Royal family is a heavy burden, and it is dragging Aethelred down. Bishop Swithun finds it funny that all the royal children share the name 'Aethel' except me; it means noble and he thinks I'm the most noble of all. "It is easier to be noble in name than in nature," he has often told me.

Bishop Swithun has good reason to dislike King Aethelbald as he taught my father from a young age and became one of his most loyal and trusted advisors. He was horrified by the way Aethelbald stabbed my father in the back, snatching the crown of Wessex from him and banishing us to the east. The king's marriage to his own stepmother only added to the bishop's anger. He is convinced that there is nothing the king wouldn't do to strengthen his grip on Wessex.

Godric reluctantly agreed to read the epic poem Beowulf tonight. I was hoping that the warrior's great feats would inspire me tomorrow at sword school. But the version Godric read out was sadly lacking in blood and gore. In Godric's version, the beast Grendel agrees that he has sinned and offers to help rebuild the village he destroyed.

August 22nd

Wulfric and Wulfstan looked exactly as I imagined them: strong as oxen, with thin beards sticking to their square jaws and coalblack hair. They were more men than boys, taller by at least a head than the rest of the sons of thanes. They stared at Aethelred and me with their dark, devilish eyes, saying nothing but letting us know exactly what they thought of us.

These boy-beasts are built for battle and they were the best at everything. They ran faster and further than we did, lifted heavier logs than the rest of us and they were better shots with the crossbow.

Osric gathered us together in a forest clearing and told us we were to practise our swordcraft. It came as no surprise when he paired brothers against brothers. The Wolf twins' swords may have been wooden, but in the hands of such brutes, they were dangerous enough to wound.

Each boy stood opposite his opponent: Aethelred stood head to chest with Wulfric, I stood head to waist with his brother. Osric shouted and the fighting began. Wulfstan lunged at me, his wooden sword stabbing the air where I was a moment ago. I span round and prodded his back with the end of my sword, as we had been instructed to. Wulfstan however, wasn't playing to these rules. He lifted his tunic and showed me the small seax knife behind his belt. He ran his finger across his throat, indicating just what he was going to do with it.

He came at me again, the tip of his wooden sword leading the way. He slashed at my head, slicing hairs as I ducked beneath. I fixed my eyes on his sword, thinking that its movements would signal his attacks. That was a mistake. He kicked my legs away and sent me crashing to the ground. Breath was sucked from my body. I tried to rise but was pinned down by Wulfstan's elbow. He held the seax knife to my throat, its sharp edges cutting into me.

"Think you're better than the rest of us, do you?" he snarled. "Think again. You're nothing – just the Royal runt."

Wulfstan was too strong and heavy – I couldn't get him off. He was squeezing the life from me and there was nothing I could do about it. Behind him, I saw something move within the woods. I thought it must be the devil, coming to claim me. Over Wulfstan's shoulder, I saw a boot fall. The weight lifted, and I could breathe again. Wulfstan knelt beside me, holding his chest and spluttering for air. Aethelred's hand hung above me; I took it and he pulled me to my feet. My brother had saved me.

"That will be enough for today," Osric said, looking down in disgust at his two sons who were both lying on the ground. "You fight again tomorrow. Same partners – different swords."

Many boys muttered their surprise.

"The king's orders," Osric said. "The Danes are coming closer and we may need every man and boy to fight. Wood is only good for fires."

Bishop Swithun was right: Godric does know much of the world, he is a skilled leech and knew how to heal my cuts. I lay in the bath, steam hiding the monk from me, a thick river of buttery-blue woad trickling across my throat and down my neck.

"If you can't be faster with your sword," Godric said, "you need to be faster with your mind. That is how you beat him. And if all else fails, look to the heavens, you'll find the help you need up there."

I looked out of the window at the blood-red sky, wondering what he meant. I lay in the blue bath water, croaking my diary entry to Godric, feeling anything but great.

August 23rd

Last night, I tried to sleep but every time Hilda scratched her talons on the cage it reminded me of my fight with Wulfstan. Before the cock crowed, I was out of bed and in the chapel, knelt in prayer over my most precious relic, a piece of Christ's cross, given to me by the Pope. My prayer was disturbed by the groan of the heavy oak door behind me.

"You're here earlier than usual," Aethelred called out, already dressed for school. "Mind if I join you? I think I need a good few prayers to help me through this day."

We knelt and prayed together. At least, I tried to pray – I'm ashamed to say my mind was out on the battlefield.

"Aethelred," I began, repeating his name until he broke from prayer. "Godric says I should look to the heavens if I want to beat Wulfstan. What do you think he means by that?"

My brother didn't say I was being stupid but the look on his face said as much: "You're doing it right now little brother," he said, pointing at the large wooden cross which hung high above us.

"And Bishop Swithun says you're the wisest of us all!" I wasn't so sure, but I kept my doubts to myself. I felt terrible for not telling Aethelred about the diary as I have never kept a secret from him. He is older than me and more likely to become king, so perhaps he is also writing a diary and keeping the same secret. However, he can't write either, and he doesn't have his own monk.

By the time we left the chapel, the soft glow of the sun was piercing the indigo sky.

"A beautiful day to die," Aethelred said. He looked at me and smiled. I didn't find this funny at all.

We were the last boys to arrive at the clearing. Most were practising with their wooden swords, thrusting and slashing the air, but not the Wolf twins. Wulftstan and Wulfric were naked from the waist up, sweat glistening off their muscular bodies as they lifted huge boulders above their heads.

Aethelred and I practised together. My wooden sword felt as heavy as a tree trunk, so I was unable to stop my brother's sword banging into my leather helmet.

"Just trying to knock some sense into you," I think he said. I shook my head to steady my vision and saw the Wolf twins laughing at me. Osric called us all together: "Put down your toys boys."

Each of us went and collected a round wooden shield and a shining steel sword.

The weapons felt very heavy compared to the wooden one.

"You're to take your turn to fight in pairs with the rest watching and learning," Osric explained. "The first to draw blood wins. Wulfstan and Alfred are up first."

Wulfstan stood opposite me, slashing and slicing the air with his gleaming long sword. "Big brother can't save you

this time," he snarled.
I looked back at Aethelred. He looked as scared as I felt. The boys had formed a silent circle around us. Even the horses were watching us.
"May the best man – or boy – win," Osric laughed, winking at his son. "Now FIGHT!"
Wulfstan threw his shield to the ground and came running at me, the cheers from the circle urging him on. I ran around the edge of the circle and then stopped, the sun now beating onto my back. I held my shield out in front of me; I could see my brother's reflection shaking in its silver rim.

Again, Wulfstan came at me, his sword leading the way, slashing wildly. I felt the air brush my face, as I danced away from the blade. He wiped the sweat from his head and lunged at me again, thrusting his sword towards me. I lifted my shield to cover my face and closed my eyes; a thunderous noise like a felled tree opened them. Wulfstan's wild eyes stared through the split his sword had made. He fell back as the sword came free from the shield. He rose to his feet and charged at me again, sweat now trickling into his eyes.

The blood-seeking beast bounded towards me, frantically thrashing his sword. I span away from him, feeling the warmth of the sun on my neck. Again and again he lunged, and again and again I spun away from him, always to face him with the sun behind. Now he was panting, and he was tiring. If he can't draw breath, he can't draw blood, I thought. With his brother's curses ringing in his ears, Wulfstan came again. He squinted as he tried to find me in the bright sunlight, swinging his sword blindly, sweat dripping from him. He swung again and for the last time as his sword flew from his sweaty hand and thudded into a tree behind me.

Now he was only fighting for breath. He staggered back towards the screaming circle, exhausted by his efforts. He swung his arms towards me, hoping they could do what his sword couldn't, but with his eyes full of sun and sweat, they were no threat. He could fight no more, his hands barely strong enough to wipe the sweat from his eyes. The circle of boys fell silent as I raised my sword. I angled my blade to catch the sun and shone it straight into Wulfstan's eyes, blinding him and sending him reeling back towards his brother. I kicked the lumbering beast in the knees and sent him crashing into Wulfric. Together they fell back, scattering the horses before falling into a steaming pile of horse muck.

Most of the circle cheered. My brother ran from it and hugged me. "You did it," he gushed. "You beat him and without any help."

I didn't correct Aethelred, but I had been helped. Godric's wise words rang in my ears like church bells when I looked up to the bright sun. I had looked to the heavens and I had won.

August 24th

My voice is shaking as I speak these words. From my bath, I am staring into the fire beside Godric, telling the monk just how close I came to death today. Much of what happened is missing from my mind, but I will do my best to remember.

Osric informed us that today's lesson was swimming which pleased me: it was a really hot day and it would be great to cool off in the water. Also, I felt safer in the water knowing that there were no swords and knives in there with me. We stood along the edge of the river, each of us stripped to the waist, awaiting our instructions. Osric stood between his two sons.

"You could do with a good wash in the river," he said to them, "you still smell of horse muck."

I wished he hadn't said that: I could feel their anger burning from their black eyes. Osric explained the lesson with his eyes fixed on his sons.

"There are no rules. It's every boy for himself. Swim!"

The boys splashed in and began to swim away. I looked at Wulfric and Wulfstan - still standing on the riverbank, waiting. Aethelred and I jumped together into the water, turning back on landing to watch the Wolf twins leap in.

Aethelred looked back at me, a flash of panic in his eyes. "Swim Alfred," he cried, before his head disappeared beneath the water and he began to kick away. I thrust my face into the murky river and swam hard. Soon I passed Aethelred and kept swimming. I turned around: close behind him were two heads, each emerging from the water like serpents, their fire-bright eyes glaring ahead.

Aethelred could see the fear on my face. I watched helpless, as he was pulled beneath the water, his arms flailing in a frenzy. I swam towards him but by the time I reached him, he was sinking like a stone towards the riverbed. I stuck my head down beneath the water and began to pull towards him but was instantly dragged back. Wulfric's strong hands held my legs tight and I was being dragged away from my brother. I did all I could to kick Wulfric off, but I didn't have the strength to free myself.

I watched in despair as Aethelred's limp body floated, face down, thrashing my arms and legs in a last frantic attempt to reach him. I jerked back – my wrist had been grabbed – I turned to see Wulfstan grinning madly at me, his hand on mine, pulling me down. Now both brothers held me. Wulfstan's free hand cut through the water and struck me on the head plunging me into darkness…

Blurred shapes moved above me. I shook the water from my eyes, coughed the water from my chest then managed to sit up. Three cloaked figures were running into the woods. I tried to rise to my feet but instantly fell back to the floor, coughing up more of the river. Aethelred lay beside me, his body turned to one side, his face towards me, water dripping from his mouth.

I managed to lift myself to my knees and tried to shake life back into my brother. To my great relief, he coughed and spurted water from his mouth.

"What happened?" he spluttered. "Who pulled me from the water? And where did that thing around your neck come from?"

I looked at the oval amber amulet which hung heavy around my neck. I didn't know; I couldn't answer any of my brother's questions. I still can't.

Eating with my brother and Judith was the last thing I wanted to do but they insisted, and you don't say no to the king. Judith was horrified to hear about my brush with death, her face twisted with anger when I told her what had happened.

"You won't need to worry about those two brutes," she assured me, "I can promise you that." I took a long look at her piercing amber eyes and believed her.

"Show them the amulet," Aethelred said, much to my horror. I hesitated, before reaching beneath my tunic.

"It's beautiful," Judith said, as soon as I revealed it. Aethelbald looked up from his plate. His face instantly drained of colour and his glass jar slipped from his hand, shattering upon the stone floor. We all looked at the king, but he couldn't take his wide eyes of the amulet. He didn't speak; he just stood up and walked away, glass crunching beneath his boots.

September 3rd

I had to wait a week before I could ask Bishop Swithun about the amulet. He was sat in the corner of my room talking to Godric when I returned from my morning hunt in the marshes.

"I came as soon as I heard," the bishop said, leaving his chair to hug me. After some time, he pulled himself free and continued: "I was with King Aethelbehrt in Canterbury. He's as concerned as me. He told me to come at once to see that you are safe."

"It's great to see you Bishop," I told him, "but it seems I already have a guardian angel," I explained, pointing towards the amulet on the table.

"So it would seem," he said, picking up my mysterious gift and examining it closely.

"Have you seen one like it before?" I asked him.

"No…no. Not one as fine as this," he said softly.

"I think Aethelbald has," I told him. "His face looked like sour milk when he saw it."

The bishop looked up from the amulet: "The king has the weight of the world on his shoulders Alfred. He is convinced that the Vikings are about to attack Wessex."

Both he and Godric crossed themselves at the mention of the Vikings. The bishop led me over to the window. "Your brother has finally agreed to build walls around the minster," he said, looking down at the large group of men beneath us. "You have seen the walls in Rome Alfred. We need walls like that to protect the treasure of Wessex."

October 4th

Little has happened this last month which is good as it has given Godric the chance to get some sleep and make more ink and writing paper. It certainly hasn't been quiet though – not with the builders hammering and cursing beneath my window. They still have a long way to go though: if the Danes came today, it would take them a long time to walk around the wall, but only a moment to walk over it.

Bishop Swithun insisted that I attend court today. As a young royal from Wessex, I sit with the witan, the king's council, and listen as the wise and wealthy of Wessex sit in judgement. It was a most rewarding morning for the king: thanes and earldormen lined up to pay tribute, exchanging coins, gold, swords and silks for the right to keep their lands. The nobles joined the Royal Family and witan for lunch, eating the flavoured meats and drinking the finest Frankish wines which they had paid for. It always concerns me that the men drinking glasses of wine at lunchtime are the same men deciding a man's fate in the afternoon.

For many of the witan, listening to a man's crimes and deciding his punishment is entertainment; they take great pleasure in ordering huge fines or violent punishments. I'm sure all the accused hated the fact that Bishop Eahlstan was there as he is all that Bishop Swithun isn't. He has fought alongside the king many times and has sent many a Viking to Valhalla – the heathen's heaven. It was this bishop who had united with Aethelbald to drive my father from Winchester (which gave me more reason to hate him).

Each man was dragged before the witan: Bishop Eahlstan urged the council to chop off hands, Bishop Swithun reminded the king that these hands may be needed to defend the kingdom. Most criminals left knowing they were to lose all their gold and one or more of their fingers.

Four men dragged the final criminal in. I couldn't see his face but I could hear his screams and curses. Each man held an ankle or wrist, stretching out their victim who kicked and cursed like a trapped animal. The good men of the witan laughed in amusement – they were enjoying this performance. The guards hurled the wretched creature at the king's feet and then backed away to tend their bruises. The criminal lay face down, fighting for breath. I stared at the scars on his shaven head. Mutters spread amongst the witan when he rose to his feet. They weren't staring at a man, but a thin boy in a monk's habit. He was only a little older than me. Trickles of blood ran down his muddy face.

"Why has a boy been brought before a king?" my brother shouted to the witan.

"Because his crime is the worst of all my lord," declared Bishop Eahlstan. "He has sinned against God."

I was staring with pity at the poor wretch and missed much of what the bishop said next, but I remember him explaining that the boy had been sold to the monastery by his father and had refused to be taught by the monks. Instead he had attacked them many times, running away with stolen gold on the last occasion.

Bishop Eahlstan wanted the boy to be whipped and banished from the kingdom, he also wanted the boy's father to be executed so he couldn't have more sons. Many of the witan mumbled in agreement. Bishop Swithun rose to his feet and whispered in the king's ear. Luckily for the boy, the king listened to the good bishop.

The king rose from his wooden throne:

"The boy is to serve Alfred. Take him away and prepare him!" he declared.

Then he strode out of the Great Hall, Bishop Eahlstan at his ear, his astonished council whispering to each other as they hurried behind.

The boy and I looked at each other: I was happy that he had escaped punishment but wondered how he could serve me. What was Bishop Swithun thinking?

October 6th

I didn't have to wait long to find out. I barely recognised the boy who walked into my room beside the bishop: the mud and blood had been washed from his face and his tattered monk's habit had been replaced with a fine leather jerkin and woollen tunic.

"His name is Wilfred," Bishop Swithun explained, as the boy looked out of the window at the noise below. "The monks mistreated him, beating him and whipping his back. If you treat someone like a dog then a dog is what you get, and this dog bit back – literally."

October 7th

Godric seems very happy that Wilfred has joined us. He now has someone else to mix the inks, flatten the vellum and whiten the pages. I caught Wilfred reading my diary last night; everyone can read it but me. When Judith visits, she only reads about her ancestors and Godric says he won't teach me as the Bishop himself wants to tutor me. Until the wall is built however, he doesn't have the time. Maybe I should go downstairs and start lifting bricks myself.

October 10th

Spending much of my day with two mostly mute monks is now really getting to me. Wilfred has barely spoken a word since he arrived. Monks are not allowed to talk whilst eating (they use sign language to communicate) but Wilfred has extended this vow beyond the dinner table. It comes to something when the best conversation I can have is with my hawk Hilda: at least she screeches or scratches her cage when I talk to her.

Wilfred has a haunted look about him. What have those monks done to him? They must have beaten him badly. If the king doesn't punish them, I hope God does.

October 14th

I've had to send Wilfred out into the woods to collect woad and nettles as after what happened today, I have a lot to write about and I don't want him to overhear. Godric also needs the ingredients for an ointment to rub onto my cuts and scratches.

The day started like most others: Aethelred and I were about to hunt with the School of Arms and with the Wolf twins gone I was finally beginning to feel safe. As always, Wilfred had prepared the horses beautifully: their autumn coats glistened beneath the morning sun. Unusually, there was no sign of Wilfred, but he had left our bows and arrow quiver hanging on our mounts.

The dogs ran off barking into the forest and we galloped

after them, riding into the heart of the darkening forest, our horses' hooves in beat with the barking hounds. Aethelred raced ahead, his majestic mount threading through the trees like a needle in silk. Then everything changed: Aethelred began to slip from the saddle, his body leaning to the right, his horse galloping to the left, ignoring his rider's screams. I kicked my horse in the belly and raced towards my brother, desperate to reach him before he slid to the ground. As I neared Aethelred, I could see the leather straps flapping beneath his loose saddle.

I was almost with him now and shouted to him, but as I did, my saddle too began to slip from beneath me and I found myself falling to the side, fighting to control my mount. Both horses raced on through the forest, the thick branches missing them but whipping our arms and faces.

I was beside him now, he was hanging to the right, me to the left. He had slipped so far that his arm was dragging along the floor, blood trickling from it. I reached out to grab him with my left arm whilst trying to steady my horse with the right. My horse jerked and my hand slipped from the reigns, only my brother's grip keeping me from falling to the forest floor. With all his strength, he pulled me up towards him, our horses were galloping together like a wild two-headed beast; I stared at their iron-shod hooves in horror, afraid that I'd be trampled to death.

The horses charged through the forest, both of us were powerless, unable to stop them as they twisted and turned through the trees and we were dragged through the brush. I looked to my brother and saw the fear on his face: we were locked together. We both knew that when our strength failed us, we'd fall beneath the pounding hooves.

The horses ran onwards, jerking and jinking through the trees. Each jolt dropped us nearer to the ground. My hand began to slip from my brother's. I closed my eyes and prayed that the horses' hooves would miss me. I slammed into my brother as the horses stopped suddenly; hanging almost upside down I looked at the bare feet in front of me. I saw a knife hang above me but was helpless to do anything about it. I closed my eyes. The knife didn't cut me. I heard it cut the saddle straps tied around my horse's leg. I only opened my eyes after a hand hoisted me to my feet. Two men stood by the horses. They were cloaked in brown with hoods covering their faces. They were wearing amulets around their necks, like the one hidden beneath my tunic.

"You should have worn yours today," said the first man.

"Or hung it around your horse's neck," the other joked.

Then I noticed the horses: both were foaming, their mouths bubbling up like boiling broth.

"Evil spirits have possessed them!" my brother suggested.

"Evil hands have meddled with your saddles," the shorter man announced, as he looked beneath one horse. He showed us the saddle straps – someone had cut them.

"How can we thank you?" Aethelred asked the men.

The taller man was patting my horse when he replied: "We need horses."

Before we could ask more questions, the two men disappeared into the forest, each leading a horse.

Aethelred was convinced that Wilfred was to blame and by the time we had limped back to Winchester he was ready to kill my servant. Wilfred looked horrified when he saw us stagger muddied and bloodied into the courtyard.

"Sorry that you didn't kill us?" Aethelred shouted at him, pushing away the guards trying to assist him. "Get off me and arrest that boy!"

October 17th

Godric doesn't want to write this. He thinks a wooden cart, on a rutted road, isn't the best place to write a diary entry but things need to be explained before we lose the light.

The bishop, along with the queen, made Aethelred see sense. He explained that evil-minded people had been plotting to kill me long before Wilfred arrived. The boy was dour faced and he was no angel, but he had no part to play in the latest attempt on my life. Judging by the way that Aethelred glares at Wilfred, I'm not sure my brother believes this.

It was Bishop Swithun who urged us to visit my brother Aethelbehrt, and it was Judith who suggested we avoid the main Roman road to Kent. Our journey along the deserted dust tracks will be much longer and bumpier, but hopefully much safer too. The king only spared a handful of men, any more he said, would attract far too much attention and make us a target for the bands of bandits who terrorise these remote parts of Wessex. So Aethelred and I are travelling to the eastern kingdom with nothing more than six thanes disguised as merchants, a monk, a young boy and a hawk to protect us.

October 19th

Godric's hand is shaking as he writes this: not because we're still rattling around inside the wooden cart but because of what happened today. He's writing by the light of the fire, against my advice, determined that should we die tonight, a record will remain of what occurred.

At first, we thought nothing of the cart veering off the track, as it wasn't the first time it had happened. It was the agonising groan and screaming which followed that told us we were in trouble. A guard pulled back the carriage curtain, the fear on his face spreading to ours.

"Run into the woods my lord," the guard said to Aethelred, "we'll hold these devils back for as long as we can."

The screams of men and rattle of horses were growing louder. Aethelred, seeing the urgency on the guard's face, pulled his sword from beneath his tunic, and jumped from the cart. I followed, keeping my sword sheathed, so I could carry Hilda, with Godric and Wilfrid spilling from the cart behind me.

The guard joined four others in forming a shield wall between us and the advancing bandits, the sixth thane lay slumped on a whinnying horse, a crossbow bolt skewering him, his blood trickling over the terrified beast. A hand pushed my head down:

"Keep low to the ground, behind the shield wall, so they can't see us," Godric urged.

The grunts and groans of men, the holler of horses, the clash of steel on steel rattled around us. Beyond them, a voice could be heard directing his men, urging them to find us. Whoever he was, he knew we'd be here.

Godric whispered to Wilfred, who immediately pulled off his cloak, revealing, much to my surprise, a bright red tunic, fringed in gold leaf. Wilfred stood up, above the shield wall and pointed us towards one side of the woods, before he ran to the other, Godric, in his brown robes, flapping nervously behind him. The same voice shouted from beyond the shield wall, directing his men towards the monk and boy, who were disappearing into the woods. Aethelred pulled me into the woods, and I watched through the trees, as a group of sword-wielding men set off in pursuit of Wilfred and Godric.

"We need to get away from here," Aethelred urged, dragging me away from the fighting and into the darkness of the woods. For a moment I resisted, my eyes pinned to the brave warriors kneeling between us and our hunters. One guard turned back to face me, smiled, and beckoned me into the woods with his free hand, before taking up his hopeless fight with the other.

Still holding Hilda, I dashed into the woods after Aethelred, the screams of men covering our crunch across the autumnal ground. I caught him and pulled his arm towards the densest patch of the forest, where men but not horses could reach. We stopped when we could run no more.

"We're far enough away," Aethelred spluttered, crouched over, fighting for breath. "I can't hear them."

"The silence doesn't make us safe," I told him. "There's no noise because the fighting has stopped. The fighting has stopped because our men are dead."

My brother didn't look up and deny this. We sat down, back to back, both trying to slow our breathing. Hilda's eyes pierced the gloom as they stared at me, pleading to be freed to the trees. Suddenly, she jerked her head to one side, and fixed it back into the woods towards where we had just come from. Our breathing was now quiet enough to hear the forest: over the bird song, I could hear the hard crunch of leaves, some distance off, but growing louder.

Aethelred heard it too: he rose to his feet and pulled me up towards him.

"Behind the trees," he whispered, "I can't run anymore."

We stood side by side, each behind a tree thick enough to hide us. Aethelred peered through the gap between the trees, towards the noise.

"Get back," I urged him, "they have crossbows."

Aethelred turned to me and smiled: "We don't need to worry about crossbows," he whispered.

Then I heard the grunts of a wild boar snuffling around in the undergrowth. Aethelred, thinking only of his stomach, pulled his sword from beneath his brown cloak, and crept towards the beast, which was busy clearing the forest floor of acorns.

"Get back," I said, louder than I wanted. "It's not safe."

"Wild boars! Two of them!" he cried in excitement. "We'll feast tonight!"

A crossbow bolt whistled through the air and a squeal of pain told me that the shot had found its mark. A second shot immediately followed, thudding into its target. The two boars lay on the ground, side by side, stone dead. Aethelred ran back towards me and fell behind the tree, a look of terror on his face. The crunching of leaves returned, this time much louder and behind us.

"It's me!" mumbled a familiar voice. Godric walked towards us, his pale face and shaven head lit by the soft evening light. His hands were shaking, and his sleeves were splattered in blood. He shuddered when he heard the forest move and crouched down beside us. Aethelred stood up to leave but was forced to the floor by the crossbow bolt which thumped into the tree trunk above him.

"Don't move," I whispered to him, putting my hand on the hilt of my sword. Hilda rattled in her cage; I placed my hand over the latch, ready to release her.

Twigs snapped on the other side of the tree. I tightened my grip on the sword.

"You won't be needing that just yet," Wilfred said, peering round the tree. Aethelred, Godric and I rose to look at Wilfred: there he stood in his regal red robes, a boar over one shoulder and a crossbow over the other.

"Hungry?" he asked.

We walked for an hour or more, in the last of the light, before choosing a place to rest for the night. Soon, the fire crackled, belching sparks into the night, as we devoured the roasted boar, all that is, except Godric.

He didn't want to eat the boar, perhaps because monks have a number of rules about what foods they can eat and when. But perhaps something had spooked him. He certainly didn't want to speak about what had happened in the woods; he just sat there shaking, gazing into the fire and slowly making the sign of the cross.

The darkness deepened. Wilfred offered to take first watch, allowing the rest of us to sleep. He sat upright and alert, on the end of a long log, looking out into the woods, with a loaded crossbow at the ready. When he saw me looking at the weapon, he smiled.

"Can't be too careful," he said with a grin. "There's wild wolves in these woods."

I preferred Wilfred when he didn't talk.

October 20th

Much has happened since my last entry. It all started in the still of night when I was roused by Godric shaking me awake with a warning. Rubbing the sleep from my eyes, I saw a ring of flickering torches surrounding us. Godric had taken over the watch from Wilfred, promising to alert us if danger came close. But the monk must have nodded off. How had he failed to spot the arrival of two dozen huge and heavily armed Vikings?

"Forgive me," Godric said to Wilfred, who immediately lifted and levelled his crossbow at the enemy.

With long swords raised and torches blazing, the Vikings moved towards us, tightening the noose. My hand trembled as I felt for the sword beneath my tunic.

"Put down your weapon my lord," Godric shouted, "it is no use against these odds."

Wilfred didn't put down his weapon, but the Vikings didn't slay us where we stood. Instead their circle parted and a man, almost as wide as he was tall, strode through their ranks. He took a torch from one of his men and came towards Wilfred. Godric pushed Wilfred's crossbow down and whispered something inaudible.

Wilfred stood stock still as the Viking yanked off Wilfred's cloak, revealing his ruby-red robes. A murmur of excitement spread amongst the men: I couldn't understand the words, but I guessed their meaning. The Viking took Wilfred's crossbow, and his men removed our swords.

"Why haven't they killed us?" whispered Wilfred.

"They must know that you're young nobles by the fine cut of your clothes," Godric explained. "You're worth more to them alive as hostages then dead in a ditch."

The monk was right as usual. The Vikings marched us through the woods, keeping their swords pointed towards us. Eventually, as dawn broke, the gaps between the trees widened and I saw a smaller group of Vikings, who had been left behind to tend the horses.

Believing him to be their most-prized hostage, the Vikings offered Wilfred a horse, which he happily accepted, grinning down at me as he mounted. I could see the fury on Aethelred's face, but told him, with my wide eyes, to hold his tongue. The rest of us walked between a column of riders who grinned wildly at us for much of the journey.

I spent that night tied to a tree, with Godric on the other side, surrounded by a ring of Vikings. I barely slept, as the Vikings snored and grunted through the night like a pack of bloated boars. At one point I started to try to wriggle free of the ropes but Godric stopped me.

"This is no time to be a hero," he said, "these cursed heathens will not kill us before they've collected their ransom."

October 22nd

We walked for another two days, at first keeping to the cover of the woods, before emerging from the trees to take the old Roman road east. It was the rain which quickened our pace: first we were pushed by sword tip to walk faster, and then when the heavens truly opened, we were hoisted up to ride as passengers.

Bishop Swithun had told me about the settlement of Vikings which my brother, King Aethelbehrt, had allowed on the Isle of Sheppey. It had clearly grown in size since the bishop had last visited. Despite the weather, it seemed the whole town had come out to gaze upon us. With night drawing in, men and women, the old and the young, lined the long wooden causeway, wrapped in their drab woollen clothes. The arrival of a string of Saxon prisoners was clearly the cause of some considerable excitement. We trotted past their whispered conversations, and through the village, beyond many turf-topped buildings and workshops, until we reached a huge hall, close to the rushing river.

Without delay, the Vikings pulled us from our horses and dragged Aethelred, Godric and me inside. Wilfred was led in by the Vikings' leader. A ring of silhouetted figures sat around a huge fire. The flames danced throughout the Great Hall, falling on the swords and shields hanging from the walls.

Through the smoke, I saw a man sat on a large wooden chair upon a raised platform. We were dragged towards him and thrown to the ground, all except Wilfred, who the Vikings thought was the most noble amongst our number. He was stood between two guards, facing the man on the wooden throne.

The Viking leader rose from his chair and approached us. The flames illuminated a silver hammer ornament which hung beneath his thick, brown beard. The light revealed the scarred face and hands of a man who had survived many battles. His voice revealed that he was a Dane who had lived long enough in Wessex to pick up our language.

"They think you are the prince?" the broad-shouldered Dane laughed, as he towered over Wilfred. "They have the brains of a boar."

He grabbed Wilfred by the hand and pulled the golden ring, my ring, from his finger. He shouted at his men and they dragged Aethelred and me to him.

"Aethelbehrt has told me about you Alfred," he said, smiling at me, and handing me back my ring. "He said that you are small in size, but big in wisdom, and that I must watch you."

Aethelred rose to address the man, but the words he wanted to say stuck in his throat.

"Let me introduce myself," the Dane said, restraining my brother with a huge arm, his twisted silver bracelets rattling against Aethelred's chest. "I am Sigurd – Viking leader, and friend of your brother, Aethelbehrt."

We gaped at the man in wonder. He was an ally. We were saved.

"Aethelbehrt sent messengers to tell me you might find trouble. I am sorry we put swords on you, but we are

Vikings – we can't help it!"

When he had finished laughing at his own joke, he clapped his hands. Four women emerged from the darkness, each holding a bundle of dry, woollen clothes. Aethelred, Godric and I immediately cast off our wet rags and changed, but Wilfred stood his ground, not wanting to change in front of us. He slipped into the darkness and returned later in fresh clothes.

That night, around their long fire, we feasted with the Vikings, eating their meats and listening to their music and poems. After many hours, the four of us, bellies full and bodies dry, were led to a large room behind a silk curtain, where we were to sleep for the night.

November 3rd

These Vikings on the Isle of Sheppey are different to the savage barbarians whom the poets sing of: songs about hard-working and skilled Vikings wouldn't be as entertaining as songs about murderous and thieving devils. The truth is, I feel much safer here, surrounded by the Vikings, than I ever did in the Anglo-Saxon court. Nobody here, it seems, wants to kill me.

Every morning, Sigurd and I enjoy a game of Tafl, and today, we played outside on a wooden table, warmed by the weak winter sun. Sigurd takes it all very seriously, wearing his helmet and chainmail for every game.

"This is our battle Alfred…" he told me before our first game, "let our minds clash…not our swords."

Our first games didn't last very long; he had my king surrounded in no time. It was very hard to concentrate on the game sat opposite a huge Dane, whose chainmail hung from his helmet, and rattled against his breastplate, every time he moved one of his bone pieces around the board. Godric warned me that I was playing a game within a game, and that it would be wise for me to let our host win. I'd like to admit that I was losing on purpose, but that wasn't the case.

Encouraged by his success, Sigurd decided that we should make the game more exciting by playing for something. To today's game, he brought a huge pile of hacked silver which had been broken up from jewellery. When I asked him where he had found the silver, he just gritted his teeth into a blackened smile, put on his helmet and made his first move. Clearly, I was trying to win back Anglo-Saxon treasure and to do so, I had to risk my golden ring.

Until today, our games had always been a private matter but with the stakes much higher, we soon had quite a crowd behind us. Well, they were mostly behind Sigurd: I just wish that the farmers and blacksmiths, coopers and turners, hadn't brought their tools with them as together they made quite a frightening crowd. I felt like my bone-piece on the board: I was surrounded by Vikings and desperate to escape.

In all my defeats to Sigurd, I had learnt much about his style and tactics, and now, with my golden ring at stake, the time was right to make use of this. His smile soon fell from his face as he realised that I was one step ahead of him; the warrior returned to the Viking, his anger increasing with every piece I took. Whispers turned to mumbled conversation behind him, until Sigurd turned around, pulled out his knife, and silenced them.

When I moved my king into the corner to end the game, his eyes flashed with anger. They began to burn with hatred when I pulled the pile of hacked silver towards me. He ripped at his sleeves, yanking off silver arm rings and golden bracelets and thrusting them onto the wooden table.

"We play again…" he snarled. "You cheated me. You stole my silver."

I decided it best not to remind him, and the growing band of armed workers behind him, that I had just won back stolen silver from Wessex. Instead, I pushed half of the hacked silver towards him and held out my hand. For a moment, I thought he might cut it from me, as did many of the men behind him, before he shook it, and strode off, two of his men collecting his half of the silver.

Godric later advised me that I should have allowed our host one more victory, given that Sigurd's protection was keeping me safe. He said that in winning the small game I risked losing the big one. What Godric didn't know was that the golden ring was a gift from my mother and there was no way I'd see it on the hand of a Viking, not even a Viking sworn to protect me.

November 7th

Today, more than ever, I feel that Bishop's Swithun's faith in me is misplaced. How can I become a leader if I'm blind to what others can see; how wise am I if I can be so easily fooled by someone so close to me?

Since I beat Sigurd at the Tafl table, things have been a little different in the settlement. By upsetting their leader, I seem to have upset almost all the Vikings, their warm smiles replaced by stone-faced scowls.

The Vikings only hate me: Godric, Aethelred and Wilfred all seem to be enjoying the Vikings' hospitality, although they don't admit to it. Of the three, it is Wilfred who seems most at home amongst the Danes. For the first few days he watched in fascination as the children wrestled and fought each other; he couldn't take his eyes of the young shield-maidens as they thrust their axes and swords at each other. I could understand his fascination: Saxon girls would never be allowed to fight like this, as much as they might want to.

Immediately after his defeat at the Tafl table, Sigurd rode off to visit my brother Aethelbehrt, the king having summoned him to discuss important matters. According to Godric, Bjorn Ironside and his Great Viking army, having raided Paris, have their eyes set on Wessex.

"It is only Jarl Sigurd and his army that are keeping the devilish Danes from our shores," Godric explained. "In return for the Isle of Sheppey, he promised to fight the Vikings, should they land their ships here. If he were to leave, he would leave all of Wessex open to slaughter."

I wish Godric had told me about this before the Tafl game. It seems that the 'Battle of the bone pieces' as Aethelred has called it, may have lost me far more than I won.

Fortunately, there is nothing quite like a Viking wedding to put people in a better mood, and not wanting to miss out on an evening of drinking, feasting and fighting, Sigurd returned looking much happier than when he left. Under a star-studded sky, surrounded by a circle of torch-bearers, Sigurd led the ceremony from upon the raised wooden platform. Aethelred had joked that should Sigurd need to make a sacrifice to please the gods, he would probably choose me. Although I didn't believe him, it came as a relief to see that Sigurd already had a bowl of blood. He dipped branches into the bowl and sprinkled blood over the wedding couple, the groom delighted to see his thick furs blood-stained, his bride equally pleased to see her floral crown painted red.

Both the bride and groom were handed a sword, which they unsheathed and held up in front of them. The groom snarled at his bride, and his bride snarled back, much to the amusement of the vast numbers of people looking on. Rather than fight each other, as I believed they might, they exchanged swords, each accepting the other's family heirloom. The couple kissed, after exchanging rings, much to the delight of the crowd, their cheer loud enough to reach their gods. The groom then presented his wife with many wedding presents, all of which she seemed pleased with except for the large whalebone, which she threw back at her husband, prompting cackles of laughter from the watching women.

"They use whalebones as ironing boards," Godric shouted at me, over the laughter, "it seems she would rather her husband did the ironing."

So, an evening of drinking and eating, drinking and dancing, and drinking and fighting began. It came as no surprise that Wilfred was happier to fight than dance, but it did surprise me that he was happy to fight with the shield-maidens. The girls pulled him from his seat and dragged him out onto the fight-pit, thrusting a sword into one hand and a round shield into the other. Encouraged by loud Viking cheers, Wilfred began to 'fight' the tallest of the girls.

"Where's the honour in fighting a girl?" Aethelred said to me, making clear his disgust.

"None...especially if she beats you," I replied, looking

up from my seat at Wilfred, who was being forced back by each blow of the mighty shield-maiden's sword.

To spare myself and Wilfred further embarrassment, I decided to end their performance. I weaved my way through the mass of sword-wielding girls, all of whom shouted at me as I passed; I couldn't tell what they were saying, which was probably for the best. When I reached Wilfred, he was reeling back towards me, his sword locked with his partner's but succumbing to her greater strength.

"Stop fighting!" I commanded. "Put your sword down."

He looked back over his shoulder at me, the force of the swords stretching and contorting his face. Again, I told him what I wanted and this time he moved to the side, pulled his sword away from the girl's, sending the feisty female crashing to the ground.

This sucked all the noise from the wedding: those seated put down their cups, those fighting put down their swords and those playing put down their instruments. All eyes were on me. Sigurd stood up, walked onto the raised platform and spoke his first words to me since our Tafl game.

"What have you done?" he bellowed, his red face, reddening further. "Why have you stopped the fighting and stopped the wedding?"

I could feel the heated stare of a hundred angry eyes on me. I knew that if I didn't get the Vikings feasting and fighting again, a Saxon execution could be added to the wedding entertainment.

"My servant is no match for your shield-maiden," I shouted, "he is bringing dishonour to Wessex."

Sigurd translated what I said, I think, which made some Vikings laugh but more hiss their anger. None hissed louder than the ring of sword-wielding shield-maidens around me.

"Why do you say this?" Sigurd said, "because she is servant?"

"No," I laughed, chuckling at Sigurd's mistake, "because she is a he…no Saxon boy should fight a girl…and lose," I added, trying to lighten the mood. It worked even better than I could have hoped for: Sigurd's translation was met by a roar of laughter that only stopped when their leader spoke again.

"Not so wise Alfred," he chuckled. "You cannot see what all see."

I turned to look at Aethelred. He shrugged his shoulders, looking as confused as me. Godric however, looked most uncomfortable, embarrassed even, for he seemed to know what Sigurd was talking about.

Words failed me, so Sigurd spoke again: "Your boy…" he said, jumping of the platform to land beside Wilfred, "…is a girl!"

The Vikings roared uncontrollably, not needing a translation this time. My eyes fell first on Wilfred and saw the burning fury on his face; then they fell on Sigurd to see the tears of laughter roll down his cheeks. They were still on him when Wilfred's fist thumped into his face. So strong was the punch, that the huge Viking was knocked to the ground. The crowd fell silent but unleashed their loudest laugh yet when their laughing leader rose to his feet. Like me, he looked to find Wilfred, but he had fled through the crowd.

"Now my shield-maiden has no one to fight," Sigurd roared at me, silencing the laughter. "Now you will fight and see that Vikings girls fight good."

The shield-maiden held her sword aloft in both muscular arms, sweat dripping from her armpits onto my feet. "Are you sure you wouldn't prefer a game of Tafl?" I asked her.

Godric wanted to write about my fight with the girl but I see no need – let's just say that by the end my pride hurt more than my body. The conversation I had with my servant is much more important.

Eventually I found him, or rather her, in the woods, doing to a tree what she wished she could do to Sigurd. When she turned around, the anger etched on her face told me she wouldn't mind slicing me in two as well.

"It's a good job I found you when I did," I said to her, "a few more minutes and that tree might be landing on our heads."

I laughed, she didn't. I put my sword down, she didn't. "Shall we finish the tree?" I said.

She swung her sword, not at the tree, but at me. If I hadn't blocked the blow with my sword, she'd have cut me down. She thrust her sword at mine, hard but slow, shouting a word to every strike: "Why…did…you…stop…the…fight?" she shrieked, over the sound of clashing steel. "You have shamed me."

On her last word, I pulled my sword away, ducked to one side, and sent her crashing face-first to the ground. It took her a few moments to stand and when she walked away from the trees, into the clearing, I could see the tears swimming in her eyes.

We sat some distance apart on the same log. "My name is Mildryd," she puffed, her voice softer than I had ever heard it before. I had learnt by attending many of my father's council meetings, that there is a time to talk and a time to listen. With nothing wise to say, this was a time to listen.

"My father is a swordsmith. My two brothers fought for your father and died for him. But I was never allowed to follow them…not with me being a girl."

By now, the tears were streaming, cutting their way through her muddied face.

"My father took their deaths very badly. He drank too much and got into a fight, cutting a man's hand from his body. To pay the fine, he sold me. I am worth the same as a man's hand. He disguised me as a boy and sold me days before my 7th birthday. But I ran away and sought sanctuary in the monastery"

We sat together in silence for a moment, the party mood of the wedding ceremony so different to how we felt.

"So, you kept it secret from everyone for all this time," I said.

A smile spread up from the corners of her mouth. "Bishop Swithun knows, and Godric knows, and the thousand Vikings who live on this island know. Everyone except wise Alfred and his brother."

For most of the journey to Canterbury, Mildryd rode beside my carriage with the shield-maidens, behind Sigurd and his warriors. She only became Wilfred once more, when we stopped to rest, close to Aethelbehrt's palace. She wasn't happy about this, but I explained that I needed her sword close to me, and as a girl, she wouldn't be allowed to fight by my side.

Aethelbehrt's palace in the east of Wessex is much smaller and plainer than Aethelbald's palace in the west of Wessex, in much the same way that Aethelbehrt himself is smaller and plainer than Aethelbald. There is no way that Aethelbald would ride out to greet us, dressed in a monk's habit, and hug Vikings as Aethelbehrt did.

November 23rd

Today it became clear just how much Sigurd controls Aethelbehrt. At the council meeting, Sigurd had the final say in every discussion, his invisible hand moving Aethelbehrt as if he was a bone piece in a game of Tafl. Many of the conversations were about the threat of Viking invasion, with Sigurd terrifying the king with gruesome tales of Ivor the Boneless' conquest of Ireland and Bjorn Ironside's ransacking of Paris.

"Wessex," Sigurd growled, "is trapped between two mad dogs. It's a good job you've got a wolf like me to guard you."

My brother asked many questions about Aethelbald's building works in Winchester, where he is busy building a strong stone wall around the city.

Aethelred's answers were eagerly scribed by members of the king's council. Aethelbehrt is clearly eager to build a similar wall for himself. From what Sigurd says, he may well have left it too late.

Aethelbehrt informed me that when I return to Winchester, after Christmas, I will travel accompanied by a large Viking escort. "You need to tell the king of the west that he too should have Viking protection. We need dogs to fight dogs," my brother explained.

"Wolves…" corrected Sigurd. I smiled and left the room, leaving Aethelred to continue the conversation. Aethelbehrt has forgotten what his eldest brother is like: every Viking is the same to Aethelbald, he would rather chop off his own hand than shake hands with one.

December 4th

I like it here in Canterbury because I am free to do what I like: I can hunt when I want, pray when I want and can train when I want. And when I train, I no longer fear for my life. No one has tried to stab me, drown me or poison my horse. I feel much safer here in Canterbury, surrounded by Vikings, than I did in Winchester, awaiting their attack.

Aethelred is also happier here. He stays in the chapel long after I have left and Aethelbehrt often joins him. Aethelbehrt has provided my brother with a tutor so now I'm the only member of my family who cannot read or write. The king here in the east has told me I must wait for Bishop Swithun to tutor me when I return to the west in the new year. If it was down to me, everyone would have the chance to read and write. How can people be expected to be closer to God if they cannot read his words?

December 18th

Godric isn't very happy that he is writing, he says his hands are so cold he can barely hold his feather. He has a point. Every word I dictate is carried to him on a misty cloud. When I told him that writing should warm up his hands, he gave me a look every bit as cold as the weather.

Despite the chill outside, the town was bustling with activity. Danes and Saxons lived side by side, bartering and trading at wooden stalls, Vikings swapping furs from the north for barrels of beer. Beyond the stalls, children skated on the frozen river, their happy shouts and scraping skates rising over the noise of the traders. The numbers within the city have been swollen by hundreds of people on their seasonal pilgrimage to visit the Saints' bones in the chapel which has been decorated for Christmas with bright bows and ribbons, made from fine silk. Aethelred believes that it may be possible to turn these Danes away from their false gods, and towards our own. Godric is shaking his head as he writes. Perhaps he doesn't agree or perhaps he is just cold.

December 25th

Well, that was a very different Christmas Day. My brother Aethelbehrt, being a meek and modest man, wanted a meek and modest celebration, but with the Vikings in town, there was no chance of that!

The weak, winter sun was rising as we walked, its long golden finger cutting through the snow-cloaked trees and shimmering on the glassy river. Sunrise, with only the birds in the trees for company, was the best time to skate.

Godric didn't agree: "I'm too old for skating," he said, "besides, we should be in the chapel with your brothers."

"There's plenty of time for prayer," I corrected him.

"But surely you don't need me," the monk continued, his face turning as white as the snow he stood on.

"I do," I insisted, "I really do need you on the ice."

"For what reason is that my lord?" Godric mumbled.

"I need you to test that the river is frozen solid," I said. Wilfred and I howled with laughter. Godric didn't.

Wilfred was a natural, he glided like a swan on water, his horse-bone blades leaving a silvery trail of cut ice. Godric however, lived up to his name, as unsteady on the ice as he is in battle. He spent more time on his backside than he did on his skates – much to the amusement of the growing number of people joining us on the river. For his own safety, and for the safety of everyone else, I told him to leave the ice.

For an hour or so, I skated on the ice with Wilfred, almost as quick as him but unable to match his jumps, spins and turns. By now, there were many Saxons outside on Christmas morning, either watching from the frozen fringes of the river, or skating on its glistening glass top. Everyone was having great fun until the Vikings arrived.

Sigurd led a dozen Danes, all trudging through the snow, ice skates hanging around their necks, panting their icy breath towards us.

"It's time for some real fun," Sigurd bellowed, as his group neared the river. The ice fell silent, as the Saxons stood to watch the Vikings, who in no time, had swapped boots for skates and had invaded the ice.

Dressed in their thick furs, the Vikings were like a herd of deer, as they skated through and around us.

"Are you all statues?" Sigurd roared, spraying chips of ice behind him. "You must race us!"

Vikings, being Vikings, turn everything into a contest, especially when they know they will win. The Saxons all looked at me and I looked at Godric – remembering what he said about the Tafl game. Sigurd hadn't been the same with me since I defeated him on the board; it was probably a good idea to give him his victory on the ice.

So, a dozen Danes lined up opposite a dozen Saxons, Wilfred and I among them. Godric joined the many villagers who lined the banks of the frozen river, huddled together to keep out the cold. Sigurd explained that each skater was to reach the bridge and turn beneath it, to race back and hand over to their teammate, with the first team all back, the winners.

"You and me…we race," Sigurd grimaced, showing breakfast between his teeth. Wilfred raced first: he wanted to show everyone just how fast he was, and he was fast, faster than the huge Viking he started beside. Like a bolt from a crossbow, he raced off, his head down, in a straight line towards the bridge. The crowd roared their approval and jeered at the labouring Viking, weighed down by his chunky metal chains and beer belly. Wilfred reached the bridge long before the Viking, and turned, waving at the crowd as he went. He shouldn't have done that. If he hadn't been waving at the crowd, he would have seen the Viking change course towards him. The crowd shouted at him and Wilfred turned, just in time to see an extended, tree-trunk of an arm thud into his chest and send him crashing to the ice. Angry shouts burst from the banks of the river and roars of laughter erupted from the Vikings beside me.

By the time Wilfred had risen, the Viking had raced past him and was nearer us than my servant. Somehow though, spurred on by his anger, Wilfred managed to pass his attacker just before the line.

"Not bad…for a girl," Sigurd whispered at Wilfred.

"Even when you cheat, you can't beat me," Wilfred panted, pushing his way past the line of laughing Danes.

Unfortunately, Wilfred was the quickest skater of our number, the rest of us slower than our Danish opponents who were so at home on the frozen waters. They raced across the ice, puffing out frosted breath like winter dragons.

"We beat you easy Saxons," Sigurd panted in my face, his foul breath making my eyes water. "Vikings are better at everything!"

They were certainly better at eating and drinking, emptying plates of meat and glasses of beer during the Christmas feast. I learnt today that a Viking Christmas isn't that different to a Saxon Christmas: they cheered when the huge log in the hearth place was lit, probably because it was they who chopped it down and they cheered when the huge, roasted boar was carried in, probably because it was they who had killed and sacrificed the beast. The yule log crackled and spat its embers up to the rafters, as Vikings and Saxons swapped tales, and jokes. Here, in the east of the kingdom, the New Year began with Saxons and Vikings sat side by side. Let's hope that the truce will last. Perhaps it will spread to the west? Let's hope that the year of our Lord 859 will be a year of peace.

859 AD

March 4th

It looks like I was wrong about this being a peaceful year. Sigurd returned to Canterbury today with worrying news from Paris: the king, Charles the Bald, Judith's father, has had lots of trouble with the Vikings and in trying to save his kingdom, he may have threatened ours. "Charles has paid a Viking named Weland to protect Paris from Viking attacks," my brother Aethelbehrt explained, pacing up and down in the Great Hall, his council looking on worriedly.

"So Vikings will fight Vikings?" Aethlelred asked our brother, shaking his head in disbelief.

"Of course, little brother," the king snapped, and he turned to stare at a now blushing Aethelred. "Vikings will fight anyone, if the price is right – isn't that so Sigurd?"

Sigurd nodded and his face broke into a blackened smile. Aethelbehrt started pacing again. "But why is this a problem for us?" I asked, looking first at Aethelbehrt, and then Sigurd. The Viking leader answered: "Weland is dangerous. More dangerous than Ivar the Boneless and the other sons of Ragnar. They fight for land but Weland kills for money and fun. And he has many men just like him."

"I still don't see why this should trouble us," Aethelred said, saying what I was thinking.

The king stopped pacing and stood in front of Aethelred and me. He held us by an arm each and stared into our eyes.

"Don't you see brothers, with a hired Viking army, King Charles can finally attack us here in Wessex."

"If Charles pays him enough, Weland will cross the waters and invade," Sigurd agreed. "I know this kind of man."

The king considered this for a moment. "You most certainly do," he said. "Luckily, I have my own greedy, Viking mercenary to guard me from such dangers."

A mud-splattered messenger burst into the room unannounced and he soon suffered Aethelbehrt's anger. "Why do you interrupt important council business?" he demanded.

"Forgive me my lord," the messenger mumbled, "but I have an important letter from Winchester."

The king stormed across the hall and snatched the scroll from the messenger's outstretched hand. "It's got the seal of Bishop Swithun," the king said, his mood softened. "I wonder what could be so important." Slowly, he broke the wax seal and opened it. Aethelbehrt only read three words before throwing the scroll at me: "My Dearest Alfred…"

Godric stood to my side and began to read the letter: "My Dearest Alfred, I do hope that all is well in the east…"

The monk continued to read the letter aloud. My brothers, the council and the Viking leader listened to hear how the bishop spent Christmas and the latest on the defence building in Winchester, which had been delayed by the weather. We learnt too that the bishop's foot was troubling him and that he had a nasty cough.

The king was angry that his meeting had been interrupted by such a dull letter and the messenger looked even more annoyed that he had carried it hundreds of miles in such awful weather.

"Leave us be Alfred," the king said angrily. "Why don't you get your monk to write a reply to the bishop? Make sure you ask about his cough and sore feet!"

Sigurd laughed. Godric leant down and whispered in my ear: "Let's do as the king commands."

I followed Godric to my chambers.

"Why would the bishop send such a boring letter?" I asked.

Godric looked out of the door, closed it behind him and locked it. "It's not boring," he said.

Godric told me to sit down and then sat opposite me, his face pale and eyes wide. "What I read was boring, but the words on the page are not boring, although I wish they were."

Every word Godric read made me feel sicker and sicker. According to the bishop, I am in terrible danger, here in the east; there's a plot to kidnap me and Jarl Sigurd is behind it. He is now fighting for the Vikings once again and has agreed to help Weland's invasion. It's the bishop's belief that Sigurd is going to kidnap and ransom me, then exchange me for hundreds of captured Vikings. Bishop Swithun has urged me to leave Canterbury at once, and to return to Winchester, where he will meet me on Easter Day.

Godric stopped reading but we were both still shaking. I can't believe that Sigurd has betrayed me: I must have hurt him more than I thought when I beat him at Tafl. I thought he was my friend: I thought he was a friend of Wessex.

I have felt safer here in the east, surrounded by Vikings,

than I did in the west, awaiting their attack. But I must trust the bishop: if he says I will be safer in Winchester, then to Winchester I must go.

March 5th

Last night, I lay awake, thinking that every noise was the first sound of an assassin. I was trying to work out what to do: I must have changed my mind more times than Hilda sharpened her claws. Godric and I decided that we had to tell Aethelred: he could be in danger too, so he should return to Winchester with us. As he's my servant, Wilfred must return, so he will be told we're leaving for Winchester, but not the reason why. It took Godric and I some time to decide what to do about Aethelbehrt. He is my brother, but the king is also friendly with Jarl Sigurd, and therefore highly likely to alert the Viking to my departure. For this reason, we decided not to tell the king we were leaving, but to write instead from the safety of Winchester.

"I can't believe that Sigurd would do such a thing," Aethelred said. "He's had every chance to kill us." "We would be no good to him dead," I told him. "People will pay much more for a prince if he is still breathing." Aethelred decided that we should leave tomorrow, before first light, and I agreed with him. The sooner we leave here, the better. Wilfred, on the other hand, is far more reluctant to leave for Winchester. He didn't say as much, but I could see in his eyes that he was hoping to return to the Viking camp in the spring, and be himself, or rather herself – Mildryd the shield-maiden.

March 11th

It took almost a week to get back as we decided to avoid the old Roman roads and keep to the woodland paths. This made our journey much longer and muddier but much safer. With the walls of Winchester in sight, my brother and I threw off our dark robes, tossing them over Godric. There were far more guards on duty at the gate than when we left, and two more, taller lookout towers had been built, each with a bell within. Entry into the city took much longer than usual: everyone in the long line was quizzed and searched on entry, even two princes.

The size of the walls has increased, and the amount of guards on the gates has increased because Aethelbald's fear of invasion has increased. Everywhere the king went, he was followed by his bodyguards – loyal thanes with large, round shields on their backs and longswords in finely decorated scabbards. Even when the king ate, these four bodyguards stood behind him with more guards posted either side of the huge, oak door.

Both Judith and the king were full of questions, mostly about Sigurd, and his Viking camp. Aethelred and I told our brother and stepmother what we knew about Sigurd's army. Perhaps the bishop has told them about Sigurd's plot to kidnap me, but if so, why didn't they mention it?

The king wants us to return to our training tomorrow, and what the king wants – the king gets. He insists that every man (and boy) be fully prepared for the Vikings as he believes they will soon be at our walls. He may well be right, and they may well be coming for me.

I may have a large family but sometimes I feel completely alone and unloved. When I walk through the town, children stare at me wide-eyed, no doubt wishing that they could be a Prince of Wessex, and swap their rough woollen tunic for a fine linen one. They may return to their small, dark, one-roomed houses, but they also return to a loving family.

None of my family seem to care about me: Aethelbald is only interested in the size of his army and the height of his walls; Aethelbehrt cares more for the Vikings than he does his brothers; my sister Aethelswith is now Queen of Merica and has little interest in Wessex, and my step-mother Judith, on the rare occasions she visits, talks about nothing but herself. Even my youngest brother, Aethelred, now spends so little time with me. He hasn't been the same since we returned from Canterbury. Godric thinks that my brother is jealous and that he feels he lives in my shadow. Why should he be jealous of me? It's my life in danger – not his – why would anyone be jealous of that?

I may live in a huge palace with many people, but most of their hearts are as cold as the walls which surround them. I really miss Bishop Swithun: he said in his letter that he should have returned from Cornwall by now. If he doesn't return soon, I may send a messenger to find him. I do hope he's safe because if he's not, neither am I.

March 20th

There is still no sign of Bishop Swithun. My brother, Aethelbald the king, was no help at all: "I don't know where he is, and I don't care where he is," he raged. His temper is at its worst during lent with no ale to soothe it. No doubt he is counting the days until Easter Sunday. Still worried for the bishop's safety, I decided to secretly send a messenger to Cornwall. Godric thinks he might know where the bishop is.

Wilfred will ride tonight, and once he is out of the city, he will change his clothes and become Mildryd. If there are any spies beyond the wall, they shouldn't pay much attention to a girl riding alone.

March 24th

Much of today – Good Friday – was spent in prayer, and most of my prayers were for Mildryd and the bishop. Godric says that I shouldn't worry, but it's hard not to, especially when I can hear the unease in his voice. When I close my eyes in prayer, or in bed, I want to imagine the monk and the girl riding back to Winchester but instead I see them lying in pools of blood. It's hard to sleep when you see that.

March 27th

It is amazing how much your life can change in one day, but at least I still have my life, I so nearly lost it yesterday. Poor Godric was so shaken by what happened, that only now, a day later, is his hand steady enough to write. What happened at night, I can barely remember, so I have told Godric to fill in the gaps.

Easter Sunday began in the chapel, with a service lead by Bishop Eahlstan, his sermon typically focusing more on fighting the Danes than praising God, much to the satisfaction of the king, who shouted his agreement at regular intervals. During the festivities, I ate and drank with the others, but running through my mind were terrible thoughts of what may have happened to the bishop and Mildryd. If she had come to harm, it would be my fault. Aethelred, sat to my left, knew nothing about this and was enjoying the feast every bit as much as the king and his thanes. Aethelbald had really stopped at nothing to make this a feast to remember: the oak table was almost hidden beneath every type of food I had seen, and some that I hadn't. Flavoured meats, birds, fish, eggs, fruits, breads and cheeses were all lifted from golden plates, as fasting finally gave way to feasting. From the edge of the top table, I watched as jokes and songs flowed as quick as the ale and wine, the noise so deafening in the hall, it was hard to hear yourself speak. When I emptied my ale cup, it was instantly filled by a cupbearer, who was clearly following the king's instructions. I decided to try to keep the cupbearer at bay, as I feared I may well need a clear head tonight. Aethelbald however, was having none of this. He summoned two servants who carefully placed the wassail bowl onto the table, apples bobbing within and liquid spilling over the brim. It was more of a bucket than a bowl; even the king struggled to lift it.

A huge cheer erupted as the king drank from the bowl, frothy brown liquid dribbling down his chin and onto his purple robes. Only his four bodyguards, stood behind him, remained straight-faced.

The worst thing about sitting on the end of the top table, is that by the time the wassail bowl reaches you, bits of food have dropped from beards into the bowl. It's bad enough to drink from a bowl containing warm ale, cream, eggs, apples and spices, but when you add bits of birds, breads and bones, you have a truly disgusting brew.

In turn, Judith, Bishop Eahlstan, Osric and Aethelred drank from the bowl, each drink being greeted with quieter applause. By the time Aethelred had passed the bowl to me, most of those sat beneath us were more interested in their own drinks than mine. Not Aethelbald.

"You don't need to drink from the bowl Alfred..." the king roared to the feasters, almost silencing them, "...you need to FINISH IT!"

A huge cheer erupted, and all eyes returned to me. I gazed into the pewter bowl: chunks of cheeses and bits of bread lay floating on top of the curdled brown liquid. There was so much left, I could almost bathe in it.

"Let the poor boy off," Judith shouted when the cheers had finally died down. "He's only nine years old."

"And you're only a girl," the king roared, "and you drank from it!"

The crowd roared again, this time in laughter, and began to bang their knives against the table, faster and faster as I lifted the bowl. Their cheers turned to jeers as more liquid spilt down my robes and over my amulet than into my mouth. I had finished the bowl but drenched myself in the process. At least that gave me the perfect excuse to leave the hall and escape the mocking laughter. A serving girl handed me a cloth with which I dried my face, and she followed me out of the feast, much to the amusement of those behind me.

"Thank you," I said, turning back to the serving girl, who walked head down behind me.

She didn't answer but continued to follow me up the steps towards my room.

"You don't think you are coming in here," I said.

She pushed past me, opened my door with one hand and dragged me in with the other, shocking me with both her actions and strength. Hilda rattled at her cage, trying to help me.

I pulled out my seax knife and was just about to use it, when her voice, a familiar voice, stopped me.

"You won't be needing that – at least not yet," Mildryd

said, throwing off her headscarf and pulling out new clothes from my wardrobe. "Get into these."

I wasn't changing until she had answered some of my questions.

"Where have you been? What took you so long? Where is the bishop? Is he here?" I spluttered, leaving no space between each question for an answer.

"The bishop isn't here," Mildryd said, silently urging me to dress behind the screen.

"Why?" I asked. "He said, in his letter, that he would meet me here, at Easter."

"That was in the letter," Mildryd said, "But he didn't write it. It was a forgery."

I stood stunned, the danger dawning on me.

"Then someone else wants me here," I said.

Mildryd nodded. "The bishop says that you are in great danger. You, and your brother, must leave Winchester tonight. Whoever wrote that letter means to kill you both."

I changed behind the screen, struggling to take in what Mildryd had said.

"The bishop rode off straight after I left him," she explained. "He wouldn't tell me where he was heading, but he said, all being well, that he would see us soon. He has told me where we must go. He says that we will be safe there."

"And where, exactly, is that?" I asked.

Mildryd paused before answering. "It's best you don't know," she said, coldly. "Just in case they catch us."

It was the 'they' which most scared me. Who wanted me dead? There weren't any Vikings in these parts, as far as I knew, and the Wolf twins, Wulftsan and Wulfric, were long gone, Judith had seen to that.

I emerged from behind the screen in dry, clean clothes.

"You must return to the feast and try to act normal. Whoever wishes to harm you, may well be in that hall," Mildryd warned. "I'll speak to Godric and Aethelred. We will all meet back here, to plan our escape."

Mildryd must have thought this through on her ride home. I saw the sense in what she said so I returned to the hall, laughing off all the jokes. I looked along the top table: everyone was talking and laughing except for Bishop Eahlstan, his dark eyes fixed on me. He pulled them away and looked down from his high table, scanning the hall. His head stopped. Did he see what I saw – Godric and Aethelred talking to the young serving girl? Did he recognise Wilfred beneath the serving girl's headscarf? Bishop Swithun has always told me that Bishop Eahlstan's mind is as sharp as his sword. Was he the one trying to kill me? As Aethelred took his seat beside me, I avoided his gaze. He picked up his cup and emptied it.

I sat beside my brother in silence for a few minutes, kicking his left leg in the direction of Bishop Eahlstan. We both looked at him and our eyes were glued together for one very long and uncomfortable moment. I finished my cup and the moment Bishop Eahlstan's eyes left mine, I whispered into Aethelred's ear. "I'm not feeling very well brother, could you help me to my bed please?"

My brother turned to look at me, his face creased and pale. "Funny you should say that brother – I don't feel so well myself."

My brother led me behind the king and his three bodyguards, giving his apologies to Judith and explaining that we both felt unwell. The queen was most sympathetic: "Take to your beds boys. I'll send someone up soon to take care of you."

We smiled our thanks and left the Great Hall, making

our way slowly up the steps. I had lied to Aethelred that I was feeling ill – it was an excuse to leave the room – but now I really was beginning to feel drowsy. When we reached my room, Mildryd and Godric were already there, both looking into Hilda's empty cage. We began to discuss the plan, but both my brother and I struggled to speak, our words sticking in our throats.

"I fear you have both been drugged," I remember Godric saying. "Not enough to kill you, just enough to make you sleep."

Godric helped my brother, and Mildryd helped me to the end of my bed. I remember the Viking banner flapping, and us falling through it. With my vision blurred, I stood in a tight tunnel, between my room and Aethelred's. My brother slumped to the floor, before Godric propped him up against the wall.

Godric whispered something to Mildryd about footsteps. He poked at the wall with his seax knife, opening a hole into my bedroom. The monk propped me up, so I could look through it. There was a shape – I was later told it was Mildryd – it blew out the candle and fell into bed. There was a knock on the door, seconds after Mildryd climbed beneath the blankets. Moments later, the door creaked open and a figure walked into the dark room. The intruder stopped over my bed and stared down at it, before staring back at the door. The figure then lifted a cushion from a seat and approached the bed.

The attacker must have thought he was pressing down against my sleeping head. He wasn't – he was pressing down hard on Mildryd's head – and she wasn't sleeping – she was ready. She pulled the blanket from her body and wrapped it around her attacker's head, then kicked the blinded assassin hard in the chest, sending him crashing headfirst into a wooden screen. The felled figure tried to stagger up but another kick to the head sent him crashing to the floor.

I can remember no more but Godric later explained what happened. With a little bit of luck we managed to escape unnoticed from the palace. The noise from inside the Great Hall covered our footsteps and the neighing of the horses, as we saddled and mounted them. This wasn't easy: Mildryd helped Godric hoist Aethelred into the saddle, who was much heavier asleep than awake. Then he helped Mildryd pull me onto the horse and rode out towards the gate.

Fortunately, thick clouds cloaked the moon; fortunately, there was a light guard on the gate, and we rode unnoticed until we had almost reached them. One of the gate guards staggered to his feet, but before he could finish his words of warning, we had burst past him. As we rode for the woods, we could hear shouts of panic behind us.

We rode for hours, Mildryd leading us through woods and forests, the thick trees and cloudy night skies hiding us. Aethelred rocked and groaned, as we weaved through the woods, his body tilting from one side to the other. Somehow, Mildryd kept me steady, wedging me between her body and the horse's neck. She knew where we were going, and she didn't need the stars to direct her.

We only stopped once, by a gentle stream surrounded by trees. We slept slumped on horseback as our thirsty horses drank from the stream. Bird song and purple skies were beginning to announce daybreak, so we were eager to reach safety before our cover was lifted.

"Not far now," Mildryd whispered, looking everywhere but at me.

We were about to remount our horses, when the forest

floor creaked behind us. Faraway shapes moved between the trees. Mildryd unsheathed a sword. The shapes came closer.

"We should ride," urged Godric. "There's devils and demons in these woods."

A whistle was followed by a thud. An arrow rattled into the tree beside me.

"We stay," Mildryd muttered, holding her sword to her face.

The shapes, some as tall as men, others much taller, continued to creep closer. "Elves and giants," Godric whispered to Mildryd. "Sent by the Devil himself to take us all to hell."

"Is that so?" cackled a voice behind us. Godric turned to face three figures. The moon slipped from its nightgown, lighting the men's faces and robes.

"Devils and demons. Elves and giants. Never have we been called such names, and by a fellow monk as well."

Laughter rattled around the forest.

"Hello Wilfred," the man said recognising Mildryd, "it's been a long time."

"Not long enough Magen," Mildryd grimaced.

Another monk spoke: "Bishop Swithun told us to expect you, and he thought you might need these horses."

The man whistled, and two horses were led through the woods. The monks tried to help Mildryd secure Alfred to the horse, but she was having none of it.

"I don't need anything from you," she said, snatching the rope from a monk.

"Except the rope that is," laughed Magen.

April 3rd

Godric says that it took another hour to reach the monastery and another day for my brother and I to wake. When I woke, I saw an old monk, sat in the corner of a small, bare room, stirring at a cup.

"Morning," he smiled, "I'm Godwine. No doubt you're feeling a little groggy, it will take a while for the effects of the henbane to wear off."

I tried to ask what henbane was, but my throat was as dry as a horse's saddle.

"Henbane is a poisonous plant," the monk explained. "Some powder must have been dropped in your drink, and your brother's too. But don't worry – this should help you feel better."

The frail, old monk was stronger than he looked: he lifted me up to sit with his right hand and lifted a cup to my dry lips with his left. "Drink," he said. "It may taste like the devil's bathwater, but it will do you good."

It tasted foul, even worse than the frothing contents of the wassail bowl. The monk lowered me back onto the bed, and thankfully I fell back to sleep, grateful that I didn't have to taste the medicine again.

April 7th

The old monk was right: it took a few days for me to feel myself again. After being poisoned, I slept for days, but last night I couldn't sleep at all. I kept thinking about the people who might want to kill me and then tried counting the arrows as they hit Wulfstan and Wulfric, but I still couldn't sleep. Eventually, I asked Godwine if he could help me sleep.

"I have just the thing," the old monk croaked, holding his candle to illuminate rows of dusty bottles. "I warn you though. This stuff will make what I gave you last week taste like the finest mead."

For a moment I considered a sleepless night, but decided against it, and swallowed from the wooden spoon. The taste was so awful that I spat it straight out.

"Thanks," Godwine said, wiping the trickling liquid from his face. "It has a rather unique taste – wouldn't you say?"

I coughed in agreement and wiped the tears from my eyes.

"There is another way," the monk said, picking up a long, sharp, shining dart. "I can dip this into the potion and stick it into your arm. You'll be asleep in seconds."

"Give me another spoonful," I said.

I staggered into the hall just in time for dinner having slept through breakfast and lunch. The monks were eating in silence, using hand signals to communicate, the only noise that of the small group of musical monks, singing softly in harmony. I sat in the seat saved for me, between Aethelred and Godric. My brother whispered, but I shook my head; our conversation would have to wait until the silent supper was over.

After dinner, in Aethelred's room, we agreed that Bishop Eahlstan was probably behind the attempt on my life. He was known for his brutality and stared at me almost throughout the feast.

"It may not have been his hand," Aethelred said, "but it was almost certainly his mind behind the attack."

This thought was as hard to swallow as Godwine's medicine. The bishop was very close to the king. Did my eldest brother, King Aethelbald, want me dead? Was he really that twisted a branch? Since the attempt on our lives, Aethelred and I had become friends again. It seems that he is no longer jealous of me. I almost think that he's pleased that someone thinks he is important enough to kill.

Another thought troubled me: "Surely Bishop Eahlstan knows about this monastery. He may come looking for us."

"This monastery was closed down years ago," Mildryd explained. "Bishop Swithun asked some monks to secretly re-open it. He says that we can trust them all."

"You don't seem convinced," I said, catching the doubt in Mildryd's voice.

She said nothing. Mildryd has refused to dress as a young monk again, she said that she had saved us and brought us here as a girl and she will remain a girl from now on.

May 10th

We have been here a month now and with every day that passes, I feel a little safer. Perhaps Bishop Swithun is right – this monastery may still be a secret. He certainly chose a good location: the monastery is hidden in the heart of the forest, with large vegetable gardens, fields of cattle and pigs, and a fish-filled river, all behind a tall stone wall. There is little reason to pass beyond the walls, except for boredom that is. My brother and I, against Godric's advice, hunt in the woods most mornings, before spending the rest of the day in prayer or at sword-school. Bishop Swithun told the monks that they need to learn how to fight so that they can defend my brother and I, should the time come. Some of the monks have refused to fight, putting their faith in God, but most have taken up the sword or the bow. Aethelred and I have now turned from pupils to teachers, trying to turn the monks into a fighting force. We have a lot of work to do; many aren't strong enough to hold a sword or pull a bow, and those with the strength lack the instinct to kill.

Godric the unsteady lives up to his name: his arrows land everywhere except where he wants them to. Let's hope we don't need to fight anytime soon.

Mildryd is happy again. When my brother and I are away, she leads the sword-school. Today, on my return from hunting, I looked on amused as two dozen monks copied the sword strokes of a young girl.

Mildyrd knew Magen from her time at the last monastery. Bishop Swithun, it seems, chose him to help us because he was one of the few monks who showed Wilfred, as he was then, kindness. However, Mildryd hasn't forgiven the fact that he allowed the beatings to continue, and so she took revenge on the monk, humiliating him at school, kicking him to the ground and holding her sword to his throat. Should anyone try to find me, they will have to fight their way past Mildryd first.

May 21st

Some days I feel like these walls are imprisoning me. Much of the day is spent in prayer or training, but for the rest, I am left with nothing to do but think and thinking too much makes me worry. I have no idea what is going on beyond these walls. If the Vikings invaded Wessex, I would be the last to know about it. If news doesn't reach me soon, I will ride out to find it.

June 3rd

News finally reached me today, but in a way, I wish it never had. I was woken by a loud knock on the inner gate. I watched from my window as a short conversation between two monks and a cloaked rider ended with the gate being opened. The rider was led into the courtyard and the gates were quickly bolted shut behind him.

The rider was led inside the monastery and up the steps towards my room. I reached under my bed, grabbed my sword and stood in the dark, far away from the window. My door creaked open, I heard booted feet enter, and a candle was lit.

"Not quite as grand as your bedroom at the palace is it Alfred?"

I put my sword down. There was no mistaking Bishop Swithun's voice.

We embraced. He seemed as pleased to see me as I was to see him.

"You'd better wake your brother and Mildryd," the bishop said, the warmth leaving his voice. "This concerns them too."

I didn't need to. Aethelred burst into my room, brandishing his sword, quickly followed by Mildryd, who held a dagger in each hand. "You won't be needing those just yet," the bishop said.

We listened in silence, sat close to the light of the fire, as the bishop brought news from beyond the walls. "King Aethelbald has been in a terrible rage since you fled Winchester. He has been sending his men out to find you. Whether to help you or kill you, I cannot be certain."

The bishop pulled a rolled parchment out from beneath

his cloak and handed it to me. He spoke as I began to unroll it: "They look little like either of you," the bishop said calmly. "And the reward of a hundred gold pieces hasn't loosened any tongues… yet."

Aethelred looked as shocked as I felt.

"Bishop Eahlstan and an army of thanes have been scouring the towns and villages, ransacking houses and halls to find you. They have even visited the monastery where Mildryd used to live."

Mildryd picked up her daggers again: "Hope they killed all the monks," she said, through gritted teeth, her face as angry as her voice.

"I'm pleased to say they didn't, but they may well have done so, had they found what they were looking for," the bishop added, coldly.

"So, we should be safe here, at least for now," Aethelred said, sat down on my bed, placing his sword beside him.

"Perhaps," the bishop said, lacking the confidence we all wanted to hear. "It seems that the king's men have given up searching for you."

"That's great," my brother said, standing up. "I'm going back to bed."

I grabbed my brother by the arm; I knew that the bishop hadn't ridden through the night, and risked revealing our location, to bring us good news.

The bishop looked at Aethelred first, then me, before settling his eyes on Mildryd.

"I wish it was great," the bishop replied, his voice soft and laced with worry. "It seems the king, or whoever has his ear, is taking a different approach. Rather than hunt you, he wants to trap you. He thinks you will come to him."

"And why would we do that?" Mildryd snapped,

forgetting herself and who she was talking to. Aethelred was about to put her back in her place, before the bishop stopped him.

"It's a good question my dear," the bishop said, his voice and head both dropping lower. "There are to be trials in your town Mildryd, the day after tomorrow."

"Nothing unusual about that," Aethelred said.

"No...except that Bishop Eahlstan will be sitting in judgement," the bishop said.

"Trials...and executions," my brother added. "The poor souls."

"But why would that make us go?" Mildryd asked.

"Because...one of the accused is your father Mildryd. He denies injuring an ealdorman in a swordfight. Apparently, he cut off the hand of a rich nobleman, and that hand is worth a lot more than he can pay."

Mildryd repeated her question. Her father had sold her and she'd fled to the monastery for her own safety - but she was anything but safe there.

Aethelred, unaware of this, tried to reason with her: "He will have to endure trial by ordeal Mildryd. He will suffer the most agonising pain."

Mildryd said nothing, she just stared at me. I knew what she was thinking: she blamed her father for all the pain she had suffered; she wanted him to feel the same.

"He's your father Mildryd," the bishop said. "God teaches us to forgive. We must try and help him. He's an innocent man."

"I agree with you bishop," my brother said, "but we can't save all the innocent men. Besides, it's a suicide mission. They will all be waiting for us. It's a trap. They will catch us for sure."

"Not if we have a plan," I said.

We spent another hour talking and planning. I told Godric what we had discussed, and what we had planned, but we both decided that it is wise to only have the plans in our head, and not on paper. It is most unlikely that there are spies in the monastery, but the reward of gold can change men.

We had to tell Magen the plan, well, at least some of it; we need the monks and they do little without Magen's approval. He liked the plan; I answered his questions and then he went to instruct the monks.

I watched from my window as they practised their part in the courtyard. Let's hope that practise makes perfect because if they perform like that tomorrow we have no hope. If everything goes to plan, then we should all be a lot safer.

June 6th

Everything didn't go to plan. I had thought the plan through a hundred times, trying to consider every possible action and outcome, but there is no way I could have predicted the day's incredible events. Even now, I can't quite believe what has happened.

The day started well: we left the monastery cloaked by the last of the night, to make the long ride to Mildryd's town. For hours we kept to the cover of the forest until we reached the edge of the town. We were too far away to see but close enough to hear the dozens of people beyond the trees. I felt a hand on my shoulder and turned around to see Bishop Swithun. His voice sounded more confident than his face looked:

"Good luck Alfred, may God be with you. If all goes well,

we will meet you back at the monastery with our special guests."

I shook his firm hand and Godric's unsteady hand and gave my horse over to Aethelred to look after. "Are you sure about this plan of yours?" my brother whispered. "There's a lot that could go wrong. Is it worth risking a prince's life to save the life of a swordsmith?"

I smiled and nodded, careful not to show my doubts. Mildryd and I left them behind, lifted our hoods to hide our heads, and walked off through the trees, before joining the thin stream of townsfolk and peddlers walking the muddied tracks to the market square. We walked next to a large family, who were off to market for a day out. A young girl and boy toddled at the back of the group, their parents and two older brothers stretching ahead of them. The girl was chatting to her doll and the boy was slashing the air with his wooden sword. "I'm going to kill the bad men," the little boy squeaked to Mildryd.

"Good lad," she croaked, looking first at the boy and then at me.

The stream of people widened into a river as we neared the square, and we were carried along with it. Hidden beneath a hood, deep within the jostling crowd, I felt quite safe. Mildryd said she lived in a quiet backwater but today it was neither small nor quiet. Hundreds of people were gathered in front of a raised platform opposite the Great Hall. A ring of market stalls surrounded the spectators: potters, weavers, cheesemakers – each trying to shout louder than their neighbours and make their line of customers longer.

The longest line stretched from the treewright's stall: lots of impatient children stood, waiting for the wooden toys their parents had promised. When they received their toys, they joined the many others at the back of the crowd: swords were swung, and wooden tops were spun as the children played happily. The sweet aromas of baked breads and roasted meats and the sounds of singing and laughter drifted on the warm summer breeze. Much of the noise was spilling from the drinking house beyond the ring of market stalls: musicians played and poets sang, their rude songs greeted by booming laughter.

"It's busy," Mildryd mused.

I nodded. "There's nothing like a trial to bring the crowds out."

A large man turned around.

"I'm not here for the trials," he growled through black teeth, "I'm here for the executions."

His breath made my eyes water and my stomach turn.

"Enjoy," Mildryd said, her sarcasm lost on the man.

"I will," he laughed, spitting bits of bread.

He turned away from us and looked towards the band of eight musicians, each cloaked and hooded, who were now playing their pipes, to the side of the stage.

"So far so good," I whispered to Mildryd, looking at the musical monks. They were surprisingly good at this.

"Where did our monks learn to play the pipes like that?" Mildryd mumbled.

The music stopped the moment the doors of the Great Hall swung open. The crowd hushed in anticipation, so we could hear the footsteps walk up onto the stage.

Bishop Eahlstan stood on the stage, dressed for the occasion: a huge crucifix hung on his long, black cloak which fluttered in the breeze. Behind him stood a row of thanes armed with swords, which hung beneath their shiny, metal jerkins. Louder footsteps followed. I counted twenty-four guards – more than we had anticipated.

A burst of excitement came from the crowd as several black-cloaked men walked onto the stage. Two were carrying a large barrel, and each of the other eight carried huge copper kettles. Steam fizzed from their spouts and boiling water spilled over the lid. One man danced in pain as the boiling water touched his toes, much to the crowd's amusement. The blood-thirsty audience roared their delight as each man poured his boiling water into the barrel. They then erupted into a frenzy and waved their hands, blocking my view of whoever had just walked onto the platform.

"Great, it's my favourite head-chopper," a man behind me shouted.

"Is he the one with the red-beard daddy?" a little boy to my side squeaked.

"He is son, here, get a better look," his father said, lifting the young boy onto the shoulders. "Feast your eyes on Hacker."

The young boy cooed with pleasure and waved at his favourite executioner. I stood on tiptoe, to look above the heads, at the horrific figure on the stage. The beast stood about 7 feet high, his face hidden beneath a black hood except for his blood-dipped beard, which hung like a broad-sword towards his knees. His black, woollen tunic was tied at the waist, not by a leather belt but by a belt of blood-splattered ears which he had threaded onto a cord.

"It usually takes him three swings to finish the job," a youth beside me shouted.

"I wager you a silver penny it takes him four today," another man yelled. "It looks like old Hacker has been on the ale again."

He was right: the executioner was swaying on the stage,

and when he dropped his axe, the laugh from the crowd made the sky shake.

"Bring out the prisoners," Bishop Eahlstan roared, before taking his seat.

I could hear the scrapping of boots and rattle of chains behind me. A sea of people parted to allow a line of four prisoners through. The crowd hissed their hate and spat their spite all over the wretched souls who were being herded towards the stage at sword point. As they past us, heads bowed, I winced at the cuts which streaked their hands and feet. Mildryd's eyes were fixed on the tallest man at the back of the line, the only one with his head up, and the only one shouting back at the crowd. A boot in his back sent him crashing to the floor, and when he looked up, he stared in astonishment at Mildryd. He then rose to his feet, lowered his head and trudged behind the others towards the stage. When the chained prisoners reached the stage, the crowd let out their loudest cheer.

Bishop Eahlstan waited for the noise to fall before he rose from his seat, sword in hand: "These men, from your town deny their crimes. Today, God will judge them...and God will punish them."

One of the thanes approached the bishop and whispered in his ear. He walked away from the prisoners and spoke to a guard who nodded his understanding and strode off, taking half of his men and several of the thanes with him. The plan had worked – they had taken the bait.

Except the plan hadn't worked. News that Alfred and Aethelred had been found in the forest, was meant to halt the trials but the bishop was determined to satisfy the crowd's bloodlust.

He ripped a huge iron bar from the hands of one of the black-cloaked men and thrust it into the barrel of boiling water. Two men grabbed the first prisoner and dragged the screaming man towards the barrel.

"If you drop the iron bar before the clouds cover the sun, then you are guilty," the bishop shrieked, pulling the hissing, red-hot bar from the barrel and pointing it towards the cloudless sky.

It took three guards to hold and steady the man's hand. The man screamed his fear and the crowd screamed their pleasure. We hadn't come to rescue this man, but I couldn't let this happen. I looked at the musical monks, who had crept closer to the stage, and nodded to Magen, who had just lowered his hood.

Bishop Eahlstan began to lower the steaming iron bar towards the man's quivering, outstretched hand. Just as it was about to scorch his flesh, the bar fell from the bishop's hand onto the guard's hand, his scream piercing the air. The crowd sucked in air, as the bishop crashed to the ground. Hacker charged forward swinging his axe but tripped over the fallen bishop and crashed to the ground, his axe splitting the wooden stage as it fell. Two thanes ran to attend him but they too crumpled to the floor, falling on top of the bishop and lying still. The crowd screamed. More guards ran onto the stage to assist, but they too fell to the floor. Hacker shrugged off the mound of men on top of him, yanked his axe from the wooden stage and began to swing it wildly at the pipe players. He was the last man standing. His body twitched, twitched and twitched again. There was a loud thud as his axe fell to the floor, and a thundering crash as he followed.

"He has darts in him," a girl yelled, from upon her father's shoulders.

"They all do," a boy from the front shouted.

"The elves must have shot them," a woman screamed,

spreading panic through the massed crowd, which surged towards me, as they fled from the stage.

But it wasn't the elves, it was our musical monks, and it wasn't notes they were blowing, it was Godwine's poisoned darts, into the backs of the guards and thanes, all of whom were now lying unconscious on the stage. Only the prisoners stood with Mildryd's father stooped over the bodies, no doubt looking for a key to free himself.

Mildryd and I pushed against the tide of panicking people and clambered up onto the stage. Magen and his monks joined us there and helped the prisoners free themselves. Mildryd's father threw his chains to the floor and tried to hug his daughter, but she pushed him away.

"I hoped someone would come for me," he said to Mildryd, "but you were the last person I expected."

"We didn't just come for you," I said, helping the monks lift the unconscious guards and thanes off the bishop.

Mildryd's father pulled Hacker's axe from the wood and stood over the groaning bishop. "Why don't we just finish him off," he yelled.

"Good idea," shouted a man, whose hand the bishop tried to burn.

"No," I said.

"Who are you to decide?" another prisoner spoke.

I lowered my hood. Recognising me at once, Mildryd's father lowered his head and then lowered his axe.

"I once made a sword for your father," he said. He looked at the other prisoners who clearly had no idea who I was. "I made a sword for King Aethelwulf."

As one, the three prisoners bowed beside Mildryd's father.

"You are all free to go," I told them. "Consider it a royal pardon."

The bishop's groans became louder. Before I could work out what to do, Magen stuck another dart in him, and the bishop fell silent again. Some of the guards and thanes were beginning to move.

"We need to be quick," Magen said, lifting Bishop Eahlstan. Magen played a tune on his pipe and within seconds, a dozen or so monks rode into the village taking the bishop's horses with them.

The crowd dispersed. Only a few market traders remained, and they were more interested in bagging up their silver than watching us tie Bishop Eahlstan to a horse. At this moment things were going well: we had saved the prisoners and now that we had the bishop, we might discover who was trying to kill us. However, everything was about to change.

Mildryd heard it first, the loud rattle of hooves on the hard stone road outside the town. I looked over the roundhouses to see a dust cloud rising in the distance.

"We need to go now," I shouted at everyone on the stage. The monks looked scared and the thanes and guards were now trying to stumble to their feet. Mildryd's father kicked Hacker back to the ground and then urged Mildryd to run.

"Help me tie the bishop to the horse," Magen shouted.

"Leave him, there's no time," I shouted back, cursing my ill fortune.

Magen nodded. He and the monks ran off the stage, some kicking the stricken guards and thanes on their way to a loose horse. "You know where we'll be," Magen shouted, from atop his horse.

The dust cloud had now reached the town. Through it rode over a hundred armed men. Magen and our monks had fled just in time but we were too late.

Mildryd pulled me by the hand and dragged me off the stage, leading me through the open door of the Great Hall. I turned to the footsteps behind me and was relieved that they belonged to Mildryd's father. We leapt over the benches and stopped at the other side of the long oak table. Mildryd sank to her knees and lifted a rug on the floor. I looked back towards the noise outside. Several warriors had dismounted and were walking upon the stage. "Check the hall," a voice boomed. It was Osric – my old instructor.

Mildryd pulled on a metal ring and the trapdoor creaked open. A ladder stretched down, disappearing into the darkness below. Mildryd pressed down on the door. Voices approached the hall. We ran, leaving the trap door slightly open behind, Mildryd leading our escape. She stopped suddenly, and dropped to the floor, then covered herself in animal skins. Her father and I did the same. I hid beneath the skins, trying to slow my breathing. Floorboards creaked as heavy boots walked upon it. They stopped, in the centre of the Great Hall.

Now the ladder creaked. When it stopped creaking, I heard Mildryd's running feet. By the time I had shrugged off my animal skins, Mildryd was stood smiling, holding the long ladder, and looking down into the deep cellar below. She shouted down something unrepeatable, before slamming the trapdoor closed.

"Very clever," her father said, as he finally emerged from beneath the animal skins.

We could hear the men cursing beneath us. It wouldn't be long before their cries were heard so we ran from the Great Hall, following Mildryd towards the houses at the far end of the village.

We reached a row of small, round houses just

before we heard horses' hooves rattle into the village.

"This way," Mildryd shouted, running through the small gap between the houses. "Behind here. Hold your tongues. They're coming."

I held my tongue...and my nose: we were stood behind the woven fence that screened the toilet. Flies, who moments ago had been feasting in the toilet, buzzed around us.

We peered through the gaps of the wicker fence. Men on horses and men on foot were walking towards us. I recognised Hacker, his head as high as the horses' heads.

"They must be here...somewhere...," said the slurred voice of Bishop Eahlstan. Two guards stood either side of him, to keep him steady. "Find...them. Rip the town...apart," he spat.

Hacker swung his axe wildly, desperate to find a head to chop. As he turned, I counted six darts still stuck in him. A man, hidden behind his horse, tried to calm the bishop. Instantly, I recognised the voice of Bishop Swithun:

"They will be long gone by now. Alfred is far too wise to have stayed here. He will have ridden for the woods by now."

"Why...would you help me?" Bishop Eahlstan snapped, brushing off the attention of the two guards. "I know how fond you are of the boy...it wouldn't surprise me if you were helping the little brat. And if I find out you are, being bishop won't save you!"

The furious bishop was now so close I could see the anger in his eyes. The dreadful stench from the pit behind us was making my eyes run and was teasing a cough from me. I held my hands to my mouth knowing that one cough would reveal our position. Beside me, both Mildryd and her father were doing the same. I knew we couldn't stay here much longer.

"Only a fool would hide here," said Bishop Swithun . "After what Alfred did to you, he will be long gone by now."

Bishop Eahlstan replied with renewed strength: "You may be right bishop. Perhaps Alfred has ridden to join his brother in the woods. I hope so. Soon he will be trapped. They have no idea my men are coming. I want him alive."

The two guards helped Bishop Eahlstan into the saddle and they rode off. Only Bishop Swithun, Hacker and a dozen guards remained. "Search the other end of the town," he said to the guards. "As for you Hacker, I think you'll have to settle for chopping wood today."

Hacker grunted his frustration, thwacked his axe into ground, yanked it from the huge split it had made, and strode off in the direction of the alehouse.

Bishop Swithun's smiling face peered around the wicker fence. "How did you know we were here?" I whispered. "This wasn't part of the plan!"

"No, it most certainly wasn't," the bishop laughed. "It was the flies above your head. They were practically waving at you. Luckily, I was the only one to notice them. I see that you saved the sword-maker. Very good."

He swatted at the flies and smiled at Mildryd. "It must be a relief to have your father back," he said.

"Yeah…just great," Mildryd said, with far more sarcasm than the bishop expected.

"You need to get away from here," Bishop Swithun explained. "Eahlstan is right: they have found your brother in the woods. Not Aethelred of course, but the young monk who resembles the boy on the wanted poster. That part of the plan worked. You must ride now to meet Aethelred at the meeting point. There are three horses for you tied up, where we arranged."

"What about you?" I asked him. "We were supposed to capture Bishop Eahlstan and get the truth from him, but he nearly captured us! What are we going to do now?"

"I grant you that we are no nearer to finding out who wants you dead Alfred," Bishop Swithun sighed. I believe that Eahlstan is just a puppet. Someone is pulling his strings. I must return to Winchester to find out who. I will send word when I have news."

I didn't want to leave the bishop, and I didn't want him to put himself in danger on my account. But what choice did we have?

"Go carefully," he said, as he left us. "Go now, and may God protect you."

We did as he said. We ran from the town, through the upland pastures, before reaching the half-light of the woods where we found three horses tied up as promised. For a moment I hesitated: should we ride to assist the two lookalike princes, who by now would have been captured by the bishop's men, or should we return to the meeting point as planned?

Mildryd sensed my dilemma: "Those two young monks have served their purpose," she said. "Besides, they will be taken to Winchester, and Bishop Swithun said that he will be able to free them."

I wasn't so sure. When we planned this, we expected to have Bishop Eahlstan captive. With him free and angrier than ever, the two monks and Bishop Swithun were far from safe.

"It's not worth the risk Alfred. If you get caught trying to help them then today was all for nothing," Mildryd said firmly.

I knew she was right. We rode hard for the meeting point, weaving our way through the darkening woods until we reached Aethelred and the monks, who were stood in the clearing with Godric. We dismounted, and three monks took our horses.

"Where's Bishop Eahlstan?" Aethelred asked, his face full of concern. "You were meant to bring him here."

He was sat down, hunched on a log, the sun setting behind him, as Mildryd and I explained what had happened. Our recount was interrupted by the distant sound of approaching horses. The monks stopped what they were doing and lifted their weapons. They stood with swords raised and with arrows strung.

Music floated from the woods and the monks lowered their weapons. "That's no way to greet us," Magen laughed, riding into the woods, his pipe in his hand.

"What kept you?" Aethelred asked.

Magen pulled his sword from his scabbard and rubbed its bloodied blade over his horse's hide. "We ran into a bit of trouble," he said, "but not as much trouble as they ran into."

"Are you sure you weren't followed?" my brother said.

"I doubt it," Magen laughed, "I doubt anyone would want more of what we gave them."

"I wouldn't be so sure," I said, pointing back into the woods.

There was enough light to reveal a long line of horsemen, riding towards us.

I looked at Magen and watched his smile fall from his face.

"Follow me," I said to the men, as I jumped back into the saddle.

Magen looked at Aethelred for guidance. "Do as my

brother said," Aethelred urged.

We rode from the clearing as quietly as possible but it was no use – we'd already been spotted. Riding at the front, I was the first to see the ring of torches ahead, high on horses, blocking our escape. I had to think quickly. There was another place. A place my father had said we must never go; a place my father said that no man should ever go.

I yanked my horse's head to the left, pulled him from the dirt track, making my own path through the trees. My brother followed, with the monks behind him, their horses whinnying their reluctance to ride through the thickets. We rode hard, deep into the forest and deep into the night, the monks behind me and the torch riders closing behind them.

"You're not going in there?" Aethelred yelled, making every effort to keep up beside me.

I nodded. Huge, stone walls lay ahead of us, milky white beneath the bright moon. Behind them stood vast columns, almost touching the stars, and huge archways standing like entrances to the homes of giants. I rode between the gaps in the wall, and turned, my horse's head resting against a cold, stone column. My brother pulled his horse to a stop, as did the monks behind him. They looked first towards me, then back towards the torch riders, who were almost upon them, before riding into the ruined city.

"I hope they have more sense than to come in here," Aethelred said, his narrow eyes looking up at the crumbling arch above him.

I dismounted and led my horse towards the largest, most intact building. Six huge columns, weather weary but still tall and straight, supported a stone building, its dark entrance reached by eight, tall steps.

"Wait Alfred," Aethelred called. "Is it true what they say? That this place is haunted by the giants who built it?"

I turned back. My brother and the monks were still mounted, undecided about whether to stay in this place.

"They believe it," I said, pointing at the ring of torch riders, beyond the walls. "That's what matters. And they won't be coming in."

"And we won't be getting out," Godric said, struggling to climb down from his horse. "Unless you have a plan Alfred."

I led the men as far as the steps of the building – they wouldn't go further than that. "There will be devils and demons inside there," one of the monks said, pointing at the dark, cobwebbed entrance.

"No there won't," I said, "the ghosts will have scared them away." Some of the men laughed nervously. Magen organised his men to collect wood and soon we were sat on the steps of the Roman ruins, a ring around a warming fire, the light of which seemed to make the huge shadows of the city dance.

Godric sat beside me. "They will try and starve us out," he said, pointing at the light beyond the walls. "If ever there was a time to be great Alfred, it is now."

The torch-men beyond the walls, sat high on their horses, looking into the ruins of the ancient city, would have heard strange sounds echoing from the empty hollows of the haunted houses. They would have seen our fire disappear and our shadows fleeing, screaming into the darkest parts of the city. They would have heard the panicked whinnying of our horses and the rattles of their hooves as they raced from that place. They would have seen sword-wielding ghost-riders – ten feet high – galloping out of the ruins towards them, screaming as they charged.

When they saw this, the enemy turned and rode for the woods. A few of their number remained, but we rode through them so fast that they were unable to string their bows. We made our escape into the woods and rode until we could no longer hear the men who had hunted us. I dropped my sword, threw off my cloak, climbed down from Magen's shoulders and jumped to the ground.

"My shoulders are killing me," Magen moaned.

"Stop your whining," I said. "The poor horse had to carry us both and he's not complaining."

The other riders did as we did: the smaller, sword-swinging man on top, threw down his weapon, cast off his cloak and clambered to the ground, with the help of the man whose shoulders he had been sat upon.

"Did you see that?" Mildryd said. "Aethelred – did you see their faces as we charged towards them?"

"How could I see their faces?" Aethelred puffed, rubbing his shoulders. "My face was beneath the cloak."

Mildryd and the delighted monks risked a laugh. "Be quiet," I urged the men. "We're not safe yet."

We listened. We could hear the stream trickling beside us and horses breathing in the darkness. Magen quietly played his pipe and the horses who had raced frantically from the ruined city minutes before now trod calmly towards us.

"Good girl," Mildryd said, softly stroking the neck of a white horse.

Each monk without a horse, held a loose one still.

"What's that noise?" Aethelred asked, pointing into the darkness.

We all picked up our weapons. Twigs snapped as something moved towards us. Some monks mounted their horses. Shadowy shapes emerged from the trees, the moonlight revealing their woollen cloaks and amber amulets. Several monks, each with their sword outstretched, formed a ring of steel around Aethelred and me.

Seeing that the approaching figures held no weapons, I told the monks to put theirs down. Another figure, cloaked but smaller, walked out towards us. "You should come with me." It was a soft voice, the soft voice of an elderly lady.

"Why?" Aethelred asked, his sword by his side.

The lady slowly lowered her hood. Aethelred gasped. Magen knelt, as did his men. The lady wept as she gazed at me: "Because I'm your mother Alfred," she said.

June 7th

I rode beside my mother, not believing that this was happening. I had so many questions to ask, but with the threat of capture still hanging over us, I decided to wait.

We reached a small home, by royal standards, just as day was about to break. We dismounted and followed my mother down a long, narrow path, lined with small, wooden huts, in which people were going about their business. A long hall stood at the end of the path, into which my brother and I were led. My mother left us and one of her men guided us into a small bedchamber: another two men soon followed, carrying plates of bread and cheese. Neither of us ate – we were hungry for answers, not food.

Aethelred and I sat down. His memories, and those of Bishop Swithun, were all I had of my mother yet the frail lady, who walked into the room, looked little like the image I had of her. She sat on a chair opposite us, her long white hair hanging either side of a face that was lined by age.

"I expect you have many questions," she said softly.

Neither my brother nor I spoke.

"I have prayed for this conversation, and I have practised it many times, but now we are sat here, I can't find the words."

Her voice was weak and wobbly, and her face was as white as her hair. "Aethelred, you will remember that the last time you saw me was just before your father and Alfred left for Rome. You travelled with them, as far as the sea, yet didn't cross it."

Aethelred nodded his agreement. He had told me this story many times.

"Your father," she said, pausing and turning to me, wasn't just travelling to Rome to find God, he was travelling to find a new wife."

I felt sick. I had been told that my mother died early into our trip, which lasted over a year, little of which I remember.

"But why did this happen Mother?" Aethelred asked. "Why did you lie about your death?"

Mother wiped the tears from her eyes. "I didn't lie – your father did. He wanted a new wife, and you can't have a new one whilst the old one still breathes."

Aethelred stood up. His fists and his voice were shaking. "And you agreed to that Mother. How could you?"

My mother stood up to comfort him, but he shrugged her off.

"At first I refused. I couldn't stand the thought of not seeing you both grow up. But your father made it clear. He said that I had to go, and it was up to me how. I choose this way: to live in hiding. At least this way, I knew there may be a chance of seeing you again."

Aethelred turned to face our mother, his face wild and wet. "But why? Why did father want another wife?"

"I was no good to him anymore. I couldn't have more children. What's the use of a cow you can longer milk?"

I felt as Aethelred looked: furious and bewildered. More, however, was still to come. There was a question I was almost too scared to ask as I feared the answer: "Who helped father. Who else knows you're alive?"

My mother, sat once again, lowered her head. After a lengthy pause, she finally answered: "I was hoping you wouldn't ask me that."

Clearly, Aethelred hadn't considered this. He sat, slumped beside me, a ghost of himself.

"Aethelbald knows. It was as much his idea as your father's," my mother said, staring at the amulet that hung around my neck.

I felt like I had been stabbed in the stomach. My brother, the king, had seen me cry for my mother so many times, and all along he knew she still lived. Confusion, anger and hatred all came to me.

"The thirst for power changes men," my mother added.

Suddenly everything began to make sense.

"Aethelbald blackmailed Father, didn't he?" I asked my mother. "He told the king, when we returned from Rome, that if he didn't give up the throne at Winchester, he would tell the world that you still lived, and then he wouldn't be able to marry Judith."

Tears collected in the creases of my mother's face.

"It broke your father's heart," she said. "He died soon after."

"Everything worked out well for your older brothers. Aethelbald seized power and married your father's pretty young widow. And your other brother Aethelbehrt was given the east of Wessex."

Aethelred sobbed, his head slumped on my shoulder.

He felt this betrayal hardest of all, for he was once much closer to our older brothers.

"We think that Aethelbald is trying to kill us, with the help of Bishop Eahlstan," I said.

My mother shook her head: "Someone is trying to kill you both, but it's not Aethelbald," she said. "He knows where I live. He has visited me. He told me he saw you wearing my amulet. If he wanted you dead, he could have done it by now."

It was a lot to take in. The shock was too much for Aethelred: unable to contain his anger, he spent the rest of the day alone in his room. Godric keeps staring at me in disbelief as he writes my diary. He has reassured me that Bishop Swithun has no idea that my mother is alive. I hope that he is right: if the bishop has kept this from me it would tear me apart.

July 14th

It's hard to make up for five years in five weeks but that's what my mother and I tried to do. We did everything together: we walked, talked, played and prayed; we even began to read together. "You used to love me reading to you when you were little," my mother said, "it's about time you learnt to read yourself."

It was true what Bishop Swithun had told me: my mother was the kindest of people. Even after all she had been through, this hadn't changed. She doesn't hate my father's second wife Judith, she pities her. "That poor girl has fallen into a nest of vipers," she said. "I hope that she has learnt to bite back."

I have told my mother that I must travel to Winchester,

to meet with Bishop Swithun, as I learn that the poor bishop is too unwell to travel. God forbid, if he were to die before I reached him, I would never forgive myself. I'm going to leave tomorrow.

Godric is shaking his head as he writes this as he believes my actions are folly and my mother hasn't given me her blessing. She has, however, given me something even more useful – two of her men, the same two men who have twice saved my life – once in the river and once in the forest. Let's hope that they don't need to save me for a third time.

My brother Aethelred doesn't want to come. He hasn't been the same since he discovered that his mother is still alive. The lie has really hurt him, and he hates my brother, King Aethelbald, for it. He hasn't picked up a sword since we arrived here. He seems to have no stomach for fighting. Most of his waking day is spent alone in prayer; he doesn't even want to spend time with Mother.

It's for the best that only one Prince of Wessex is riding to Winchester tomorrow. Both of us are marked men.

September 23rd

Our meeting with Bishop Swithun was most unexpected, as was the news he gave me. I rode to Winchester beneath the darkening sky, cloaked in black like my two companions, believing that I would be meeting the bishop in his private residence.

My two companions rode in silence and remained so when they began to ride away from Winchester. I trusted my mother, so I trusted them, and I followed them and my instincts towards Southampton.

Southampton was once a thriving, bustling city but the

Viking raids almost twenty years ago had changed all that. Living near the sea is not so popular these days – only a small settlement of defiant Saxons remain: their thatched houses packed together, surrounded by low walls and wattle fencing – hardly enough to keep the Danes at bay.

Perhaps the smell will be a better deterrent. All manner of fish – some fresh – some not – hung from the houses, and fish oil burnt in the little lamps, their light licking the limewashed walls. Two old women sat outside, beneath the oil lamps, one grinding flour on her quern stone and the other gutting fish on a slab. Neither took any notice of us. I followed my companions into one of the small houses, the cold-clay floor, covered with dry rushes, crunching beneath our feet.

We had been sat down for only a minute or so, when the bishop appeared. He had a monk either side of him and they both helped lower the bishop into his chair. He sat beneath the lamplight: his eyelids falling into the folds of his gaunt, pale face.

His face furrowed as he smiled weakly. He held out his hand and I took it in mine.

"I didn't know about your mother," he whispered. "Your father kept me in the dark. He knew I wouldn't be part of it."

Tears trickled down the old man's cheeks.

"The king has no idea that I know," he added.

"And he has no idea that you are with her. We must keep it that way. For your sake, and for your mother's."

I reassured the bishop that my mother's whereabouts, as well as our own, remained secret.

"If there were rumours about your mother living, no good would come of it," the bishop said, both his voice and grip strengthening. "It would be bad for us all…" He finished his sentence with his wide, wild eyes.

"Your brother, the king, has more to lose than anyone else, should your mother be discovered," the bishop said, his hands now gripping his chair.

"So, you think I am still in danger," I asked.

The bishop paused. He looked at me and then at each of my two men. "We are all in danger," he muttered. "Your father used fishermen for information. They sail the seas and they often see danger first. And what they have seen across the channel should strike the fear of God into all of us."

"Vikings?" I said.

The bishop crossed himself and nodded. "Weland is assembling a huge fleet of warships in Francia. I fear that he will bring about the end of Wessex."

"You must tell the king" I urged the bishop.

Again, the bishop paused before speaking. "Should I?" he said. "Or should I just tell you and Aethelred?"

An uneasy silence followed. I couldn't believe what the bishop was suggesting.

"The Vikings cannot be defeated easily," he said. "You and Aethelred could flee to Cornwall, hide there and let the Vikings defeat Aethelbald for you. God willing, you'd come out of it as rulers of Wessex."

"Or whatever's left of it, when the Vikings are finished," I sighed.

The bishop's shocking suggestion stayed in my head as we rode home. Yet, the bishop may have a point. Why should I help the king? He fooled me and my brother into thinking our mother was dead. He deceived the kingdom. Does a man like that deserve to rule Wessex?

September 24th

I decided that I had to tell Aethelred and Mother, and when I did, I didn't get the response that I'd expected. They both agreed with Bishop Swithun. "Wessex needs you alive Alfred," Mother said. Aethelred told me he has given up on Aethelbald – he's happy to see the end of his reign. But should Wessex fall with him? When the Vikings come, why should the innocent die alongside the king and his cronies? In the unlikely event of me being next in line for the throne, who would want to fight for a coward? Wessex needs a great king – not a boy who runs from battle.

November 23rd

Still no news of a Viking attack. Godric believes that Wessex is safe for the winter: "The roads will soon be too muddy for their men, and the rivers too frozen for their ships."

I'm praying for a long winter. Mildryd visited Winchester this week, to fetch items for her father, and she has reported that the walls of the city are almost complete. However, if what the bishop says of Weland's great army is true, even the walls of Rome won't keep them out.

Mildyrd's father has taken over the forge and together they are making and repairing weapons and their relationship. When she isn't making swords, Mildryd is swinging them, teaching the monks and scores of children how to fight. Because the Vikings kill everyone: the young and old, the women and the sick, then everyone must be prepared to fight. That's what my father used to tell me, and that's what my brother, the king, believes. I'm not so certain: I think it will be words and not weapons that bring peace to Wessex, but there's no harm, I guess, in being able to use both.

December 3rd

A fisherman from Southampton visited today, bringing surprising news from Bishop Swithun.

King Aethelbald is gravely ill, so sick in fact that he may save the Vikings the trouble of killing him. Neither myself, Aethelred or my mother have shed any tears. Apparently, the king has retreated to Shelbourne, and the witan have decided to grant his powers to Judith.

"So, the fate of Wessex now lies in the hands of that girl!" my mother snapped, at the unfortunate fisherman.

He left before answering, leaving behind many questions...and the smell of oysters and kippers.

December 10th

Mother has gone. My heart sank as Godric read her letter. She feels that others may know that she lives, and with Aethelbald too weak to stop them, she fears for my safety.

"When they come for me, they will find you here," she said. So, she left because of me. Because of me she is now riding where only God knows. Godric thinks that she may have gone to Shelbourne, where Aethelbald lies on his sick-bed. Surely not? I guess there's only one way to find out. Aethelred begged me not to go after her. "For all we know, there could be a trap," he said. Godric agreed with him. "Best to not put both eggs in the same basket," he said. So, tomorrow morning, I will ride to Shelbourne, with Godric as my pen and Mildryd as my sword.

December 20th

When I saw the king I was shocked – only half of the man I remember remains. He welcomed me with blank hollow eyes, which were set deep into his thinning face. The little hair he had left was thin and grey, much like his face. I looked at him with pity, not anger, forgiving but not forgetting how cruelly he had treated my mother.

The king was without his bodyguards, so I had to help raise his frail body from the bed. When he spoke, it was hard to make out his words, as his voice was as weak as his body.

"I knew you'd come Alfred..." he whispered.

He looked beyond me and Godric, hoping to see another.

"Aethelred?" he asked in a thin voice. I shook my head.

"Perhaps he still thinks I tried to kill you," he said, his voice fading away at the end of each sentence.

"He doesn't," I said. "He has stayed close to Winchester in case he is needed to fight."

The king managed a smile which only deepened the lines of his face. He knew, as much as I did, that I was lying.

"You believe me, don't you baby brother," Aethelbald said, resting his hand weakly on my shoulder. "If I wanted you dead...you'd be dead...I am the king after all..."

I nodded. "Of course I believe you," I said, truthfully.

Roused by this conversation, the king rose from his sick-bed and walked unaided to the window. I dismissed Godric and told him to wait with Mildryd for I felt that my brother would say much more without the monk present.

For a moment we stood, staring at the snow flurries outside. After some time, the king's weak voice broke the silence: "Someone who wants Wessex, is trying to kill you, not someone who already has it."

"Everyone wants Wessex," I said. "Saxons, Vikings..."
"King Charles in Francia and Weland," my brother added. He faltered as he tried to walk from the window. I helped him into his seat, beside the fire. He looked at the flames as he spoke: "If you were only a little older Alfred, you'd be my choice as king. Father was right about you. You are the best of us all."
It was my brother speaking to me now, not the king he had become. There was a tenderness in his voice that I had long forgotten.
"What Wessex needs now is a strong ruler...one who can bring it together...you may be young... but you are the best hope we have. With the good bishop beside you...Wessex would be in safe hands."
I could barely believe what I was hearing. The man who I'd thought was trying to kill me, was saying I should be king.
Aethelbald looked at me, the light of the fire showing the sadness in his face.
"But the witan will never agree to that. Whilst I still breathe, they will be plotting their next moves. They will choose the strongest lord amongst them who has gold and lands to give...not the ruler who is best for Wessex. I fear that whoever has been trying to kill you, will have more power than ever before, and with me gone, there will be no one to stop them. I fear for your life Alfred. Take care my little brother."

December 21st

I couldn't speak to Aethelbald today. The king was unable to speak to anyone. When I entered his room, the grave faces of his doctors brought the news I feared. They were stood beside him, as he lay still on the bed. He was alive – but only just. I wet his lips with a cloth and his eyes opened briefly. It took a little longer and a little water before he could open his mouth.

At first, he breathed, then he spluttered a cough. A word tried to follow but it stuck in his throat so I reached for a cup and tried to loosen the word with wine. His two medics and I stooped to hear the word. It was faint, but it was clear: "Judith."

"Do not worry Sire, we have sent for your wife," said one medic.

"She arrives tomorrow," the other said.

The king closed his eyes and mouth again, only to open them to mutter the same word. The medics replied with the same answer. This ordeal was finally broken when, to my great surprise, the king found the strength to whisper my name. I leant closer once again, to hear the word that followed: "Go…go…go," the king breathed.

The medics pulled me to one side: "The king knows he's dying," the elder of the two said.

"He doesn't want you to see him die," said the younger. "You should go."

Godric and Mildryd agreed. We left the king; there was little more we could do for him. Godric is now writing this diary entry from my mother's estate once again. I expect news of the king's death will reach us tomorrow.

December 25th

There has been no news, so the king must still live. My brother has always been a fighter and it seems that his last fight may be his longest. With the king dying and Wessex in fear of the Viking axe, there was little Christmas celebration.

Mildryd is furious that I wouldn't allow her to train today; she didn't agree that the fighting should stop for Christmas.

"Do you think the Vikings will put their swords away just because it's Christmas?" she mocked.

860 AD

January 6th

Every day, for the last two weeks, I have expected word of the king's death – today it has finally come. It was Bishop Swithun who brought the news. Too weak to ride himself, he travelled by cart, escorted by the men we met in Southampton. His two companions led him into the hall to meet us, and there he sat by the fire, the snowflakes wetting his cloak as they melted away.

"Your brother died a week ago," the bishop said, warming his hands by the fire. "He is with God now."

It was Aethelred who broke the long, uneasy silence. "Why has it taken a week for us to learn this?"

The bishop shuffled in his chair: "Queen Judith was expected to ride back to Winchester and bring the news with her, but no one has seen her since she left Shelbourne."

The bishop sensed my concern for Judith. "She may

have fled for her own safety, back to Francia, or she may be with the Danes."

I shuddered at the very thought of it. I pictured her safe back at the magnificent court of Charlemagne rather in Danish hands.

"There is no way the witan would approve of a queen," Aethelred said.

The bishop agreed: "Yes…unless she married another member of your family," he laughed. "Maybe it's your turn next Aethelred. At least you're of a similar age."

The idea repulsed Aethelred. "Marry my own stepmother! You have got to be joking. Besides, she will only want to marry the new king, and that's not likely to be me."

"True enough…" the bishop mused, as he poked the hearth with a stick. "The king didn't recommend his successor…no one has been named Aetheling…"

He turned his eyes to me before continuing: "…Which is probably for the best."

"So, what happens now?" Aethelred asked, rising from his seat to stand by the fire.

"The witan is meeting next week. They have sent word to the east, and Aethelbehrt is on his way."

"He wouldn't travel this far for nothing," Aethelred said. "He expects to be named king of all Wessex. Well, he can have it," he added, before walking out of the Great Hall.

The bishop waited for Aethelred's footsteps to fade before he spoke to me. "Aethelred is right. Your brother Aethelbehrt will be named king of all Wessex."

"But he is weak," I said.

"And that is why the witan want him. A weak king can be controlled. A strong king can't. They want who's best for them. Not who's best for Wessex."

"Is Aethelbehrt the man to defeat the Vikings?" I asked.

The bishop laughed: "Aethelbehrt is more worrier than warrior. You are Wessex's best hope for survival Alfred. But the witan won't vote for you or Aethelred."

From the moment we fled Winchester, Aethelred and I knew that our chances of ever becoming king had gone. As far as the people of Wessex were concerned, we had abandoned them.

"The king's last act of protection was not to name you as Aetheling. Had he done so, then your life would be in danger once more. You haven't been killed, you have been disgraced, and that, I hope, is enough for whoever wanted you dead. You should be safe in Winchester once again. You and your brother will ride with me tomorrow."

The last time I was in Winchester, someone tried to kill me. I really don't want to go back, but a Prince of Wessex must attend a king's funeral, and a Prince of Wessex needs to attend the witan. I won't be named king next week, but if I want to be king one day, I need to act like one now.

January 7th

Mother returned today. I was surprised that Bishop Swithun wasn't shocked, when we saw her riding towards us, with at least fifty warriors riding under the Cornish flag.

"She's been in Cornwall these last few weeks, gathering support and fighters," the bishop explained.

"Do the men have any idea who they are riding with?" I asked the bishop, concerned for my mother's safety.

"I hope not," the bishop replied, as he was helped into his cloak by one of his men. "Only the Cornish leader knows who she really is, and he isn't with them."

"Why would Mother need these men?" Aethelred asked, looking amazed at the approaching procession.

The bishop stopped at the door and turned back towards us with a smile:

"They're not for her…they are for you two. They will ride with you to Winchester and stay to protect you. They are good men, honourable men, with no love of Wessex or the witan. So they should keep you safe."

The woman who strode into the Great Hall looked younger and more energetic than the one who had left a few weeks ago. She hugged both me and my brother, and I could feel the strength within her.

"Go to Winchester my boys," Mother said, refusing the seat I offered her, but gratefully taking the wine. "Go to your brother's funeral. Attend the witan. Listen to what they have to say. Let your head, not your heart guide you."

Confused, I looked to the bishop for answers. He simply nodded in agreement. It looks like I will only get the answers I need in Winchester.

January 8th

Aethelred and I are back in our old bedrooms, each with two Cornish guards posted outside. It took some time to convince Bishop Eahlstan and the witan to allow the Cornishmen into the palace; it was only when my brother, Aethelbehrt, sided with me, that they were allowed in.

Aethelbehrt is sleeping in the old king's bed and sitting in the old king's seat, he is king in all but name. There is little point in attending the witan, as it seems the decision has already been made. What this means for me and for Aethelred however, remains a mystery.

January 9th

Aethelbehrt is now king of all Wessex. The witan's decision surprised no one, least of all me or any of the thanes and earldormen. These men, noble in name but not in nature, pretended that they had travelled from the four corners of Wessex for the king's funeral, but really all they were interested in were the decisions which came next. What lands and honours where to be handed out? What gifts would the dead king make in his will? Who would rule Wessex?

What did surprise me is that the witan want Aethelred and I to move to Canterbury, to rule the east of the kingdom. This was something of an unexpected decision with Aethelbehrt remaining in Winchester. The witan's plan didn't surprise Bishop Swithun however, in fact I suspect he may have influenced their decision.

"It's the best thing for you and the best thing for Wessex. When the Vikings land, it will almost certainly be in the east. You and Aethelred can negotiate with them and delay them until we arrive. You are our best hope of peace Alfred."

I don't usually disagree with what the bishop advises, but I did today, I just didn't tell him. The Danes, in their heavily laden warships, won't be risking their lives on the sea, just to come and talk. They will take our gifts of gold and silver alright - but it will end in war. They will not stop until they have the land of Wessex itself. Despite the confidence of Bishop Swithun, I don't see how a ten-year-old prince and his teenage brother will be able to stop them without an army.

January 10th

Today, Aethelred and I stood before the new king, and his council, and told them that it would be an honour to serve Wessex in this way and that we were delighted to be moving to the east. We said the words, but we didn't believe them. In the last few months we have found our mother, we don't want to lose her again. She can't come with us – she is dead to all but a few people. We will have to leave our hearts in the west and take our heads to the east.

January 11th

Mildryd won't be travelling to the east with us. She offered to, but I knew she only spoke out of loyalty, and not out of want. What she does want, although she won't admit to it, is to stay with her father and make up for lost time. How I envy her…I would love to do that with my mother. Instead, once again, my fate has been influenced by others. I feel like a Tafl piece on a board, being moved about by the will of others.

January 12th

The new king has added his own 'war trophies' to the walls of the Great Hall. My father's and Aethelbald's trophies have been moved to the side to make way for Aethelbehrt's captured Viking banners and shields, which he claims to be spoils of his victories. He may be able to fool the thanes and earldormen who sit around his table, but not me. I recognise the banners and shields: I saw them on the Isle of Sheppey, in the hands of Jarl

Sigurd's men. The only fighting the king would have done, would have been over the price he paid for them.

February 18th

If King Aethelbehrt fears a Viking attack, it doesn't show. Since becoming king, he hasn't once picked up his sword nor for that matter have any of his thanes. Sword-school, which nearly killed Aethelred and I, has stopped altogether, as has the building of the walls around the abbey.

Bishop Swithun was the only man brave enough to mention this at the witan meeting this morning. "My spies tell me that a huge Viking army is preparing to invade as we speak. Should we not be preparing? Should we not finish the walls your brother began?" Most of the witan sat in silence, no doubt secretly agreeing with the much-respected bishop, whereas those favouring the king, or those wanting his favour, openly voiced their disagreement. Only when the king rose and began to speak, did they stop their mumbled musings. "My brother Aethelbald, and our father before him, were both great warriors…and great kings," Aethelbehrt said, looking around at his witan, most of whom were nodding in agreement. "But I am not like them… I am a different type of king." Now only Bishop Swithun nodded in agreement. "With every brick they added to the walls, with every arrow shot, with every swing of the sword in practise, they spread fear amongst the people. The kings constantly spoke about Winchester being attacked but was it? The Vikings would not dare attack Winchester. We are too strong. I am simply reminding my people of that."

The bishop, frail and weak, found the strength to stand. He stepped forward, the spokesman for those too timid or too wise to voice their disagreement. "The last king and your noble father didn't spread fear my lord," he said. "Every brick they added to the walls gave the people confidence. You are wrong."

Silence fell as the hall watched for the reaction of the king.

"Have a care old man!" cried Aethelbehrt in a fury. "Are you saying your king is unfit to rule?"

Two of his bodyguards stepped forward, their hands on their swords, expecting to answer their master's call. The bishop had gone too far. His words were treasonous. Punishable by death. The king paused...he didn't want to look weak in front of his council, but he was also aware of how arresting the frail, popular bishop would make him look.

"Bishop..." said Aethelbehrt, getting control of his temper again. "You have given our family wise council over many years," the king began, his voice quiet and calm. "My father always said that you were his truest friend. He valued your opinion and always acted upon it."

The witan nodded their heads – unusually for them they had found something they all agreed upon.

"In fact, my father King Aethelwulf married Judith, at your request. And once my father died, my brother, Aethelbald, married Judith, again at your request. Is this not true. Bishop?"

The witan was united in shaking their heads and mumbling their disapproval. The bishop tried to speak but his weak words were quashed by the king's: "You favour Judith? Perhaps you know where she is? Perhaps you have hidden her from us? Perhaps it's you and your supporters that we should fear?"

Every sentence the king spoke was louder than the last and greeted with a chorus of raucous agreement. Some may have disagreed with the king, but none were foolish enough to show it. The king was improving his own reputation by ruining the bishop's.

"I wonder what my poor mother would make of that?" the king cooed, lowering his head onto his hands, as if he were an actor on the stage. "Perhaps you could ask her…" he paused, staring towards Aethelred and myself, "…next time you pray for her?"

I felt sick. The king knew…he knew that my mother lived. I looked at the bishop. The little colour he began with had been drained from his face. He began to leave the Great Hall unaided, those that had helped the frail, elderly bishop into the meeting abandoning him. My heart was breaking – I couldn't stand to see my good friend humiliated, so I rose from my seat and held him by the arm.

"Leave me be Alfred," the bishop said, his eyes watering. "I don't wish to speak to you." He covered his face as he whispered: "Not here."

I reluctantly left him and told Aethelred what the bishop had whispered. When I returned to my room, Godric was there and he could barely believe what I had just witnessed in the Great Hall.

"The poor bishop. I must go and find him," Godric said, hastily putting his parchment away.

We were both alerted by the shouting which came from outside the window. I opened the shutters. Light, cold and a rush of noise burst into my bedroom. When I looked below, I could barely believe my eyes. A lone figure was stood, his back to us, atop the high, wooden platform beside the wall. Ever so slowly, he was lifting bricks from the platform and placing them into the gaps in the wall. Every brick he placed was greeted with a cheer from the crowd, and as the crowds grew, so did the cheers.

"Godric…you don't need to find the bishop," I said.

"Why not?" Godric called, walking back towards me.

"Because I've found him…and he seems in good spirits."

By the time Godric looked down from the window, the crowd were helping Bishop Swithun finish the wall.

"The king may have turned his witan against the bishop, but the people will always love him," Godric said.

It wasn't just the people who loved the bishop: The king's guards had put down swords and picked up bricks, and now worked amongst the bishop and the throngs of people. By now, the entire length of the wall usually visible from my window, was hidden behind bodies: some were lifting bricks to the scaffolds, others were repairing and reinforcing the lower parts of the wall. The bishop, a man of the people, was now hidden amongst the people.

The crowd were too busy to notice the king when he walked out to observe the commotion, and those that did see him, turned immediately back to their work. It was Bishop Swithun they admired, not the king, and they would work the wall for as long as the bishop wanted.

I watched the king, expecting him to order his men to disperse the crowds and arrest the bishop. I'm sure that's what he wanted to do but instead, much to my amazement, he joined the crowd, lifting and carrying bricks towards the bishop. He even ordered his guards to light torches so that the people could work long into the night.

"If you can't beat them…join them," Godric mused.

'Joining them today…punishing them tomorrow,' I thought to myself, dearly hoping that I was wrong.

March 5th

The people have continued what the bishop started. They have worked day and night, and now the wall is almost complete. Tomorrow, we begin our journey to Canterbury, no doubt when I return the wall will be finished.

The king summoned Aethelred and I to remind us what he expected us to do: "If the Danes land, which I very much doubt they will, they will land in the east. You are to negotiate with them. Invite them to feast at Canterbury. They have come to milk the cow...not to kill it. Promise them land…but not too much...just enough to keep them happy."

Keep them happy? Weland's men are not like Jarl Sigurd and his warriors. These Vikings aren't coming to feast, they are coming to fight and no amount of meat or land will keep them happy."

March 10th

This time, the journey east was less eventful and much quicker. We were welcomed into Canterbury by some of Aethelbehrt's guards, who remembered us from our last visit. We could hear the noise in the Great Hall, long before we reached it.

"Sounds like we have arrived just in time for a feast," Aethelred said.

"Feasting is all they do," one of the guards muttered, probably louder than he meant.

The hall was full of food, drink and Vikings. Sat highest on Aethelbehrt's throne was Jarl Sigurd, with a piece of meat in one hand and a blue glass jar in the other.

"Alfred...and...your brother...come over here...I have been keeping your seat warm," Jarl Sigurd roared, over the sound of the feasting Danes.

He stood up and offered me the throne. I declined it. He hadn't been keeping it warm – he'd been keeping it wet – bits of meat and bones lay in a puddle of beer.

Unable to hear ourselves think over the row of the singing and shouting in the Great Hall, Aethelred, Jarl Sigurd and I walked and talked in the gardens. Aethelred admired the rows of early spring flowers, their bright colours extending in long lines between rugs of the richest greens. But Jarl Sigurd didn't see beauty in the flowers, he saw danger: "Spring is here...Weland is coming," he said.

Now I saw the flowers as rows of men lined up for battle.

March 18th

Jarl Sigurd has posted lookouts along the coast of Kent and along the riverbanks. So far, we have had reports of fishing boats, dolphins and even sharks, but nothing to trouble us yet. I hope it stays that way, but the Viking leader is taking no chances.

"He is preparing his people for war. Soon, it will be Danes fighting Danes," he said.

I have this horrible feeling, in the pit of my stomach, that when it comes to the crunch, Jarl Sigurd will side with his fellow Danes. Maybe he is training his men and women to fight us? If he is, we have no chance.

March 23rd

Jarl Sigurd invited me to his war council, which is much like a Saxon witan but with longer beards and more drinking. Two of his men, both too small to be warriors but the ideal size to spy, explained that Weland was loading his ships, in readiness to sail. "We counted over sixty ships my lord," I heard one of the men explaining. The long beards of the war council shook in digust.

"Weland is bringing supply boats as well as warships." "He isn't coming to fight…he is coming to live," Jarl Sigurd translated.

"How can we be sure he is coming?" Aethelred asked.

"These men drank in Weland's hall and spoke to his warriors," explained Sigurd. "Weland's is coming."

A murmur spread around the circle. The Vikings spoke in hushed voices. A growing fear spread over me. Had Sigurd's men decided which side to fight for? Would they fight at all? Now that they had heard the size of Weland's army, perhaps they thought he couldn't be beaten. There can be no doubt that war is coming and I'm not sure that I have the words, or the men, to stop it.

April 26th

Three days ago, I looked out through the chapel window, to see long lines of Danish people, old and the young, streaming into the city, holding all that they could carry. Many Saxons were unhappy with our decision, but both Aethelred and I knew that if we didn't allow Jarl Sigurd's people into the city, he would be even less likely to fight for us.

"If we can defend his people, then he may defend us," I explained to the witan. But I wasn't totally convinced by my own words, and I'm not sure that they were either.

Aethelred and I walked through the city today to see Danes and Saxons living and working side by side: ploughing the fields, making chainmail and casting weapons, each learning from the other; children sowing seeds and shouting at the birds, or playing together in the streets, the Saxon children teaching the Danes how to play knucklebones and sharing their rag dolls and spinning tops.

"Are we so different?" I asked Aethelred.

Aethelred shrugged his shoulders. "Our gods may be... but I'm not sure we are," he said.

I hope today, that I saw a glimpse of the future: Saxons and Danes, working and fighting side-by-side. Godric is shaking his head as he writes this, but I don't see why it can't happen and if I become king, I will do everything I can to make it so.

June 3rd

Jarl Sigurd's spies returned with the news we had all been dreading: the huge Viking fleet was about to set sail for England. However, the news wasn't exactly as we expected; the spies had learnt that the Vikings weren't landing in the east, they would attack us in the west.

Aethelred told me to ride to Winchester to warn the king: "You are the fastest rider and you know the land far better than me. You ride...I will march the men of Kent to join you."

Jarl Sigurd agreed: "I will raise my army too. Don't start the fight without me!"

I rode hard for the west, with my Cornish guard and

Godric for company. Godric urged me to stop, so that we and the horses could rest, but once dismounted, I could tell that he wanted to talk: "Alfred…can we be sure that the Danes are landing in the west? After all, this information comes from a Dane."

I had been considering this thought on the long ride. Perhaps Jarl Sigurd was trying to lure me and Aethelred from the east, leaving the gates of Canterbury open for his kinsmen. Perhaps he wanted me out of the way to protect me, perhaps he was sending me away from the war rather than towards it? There was only one way to be sure: we would ride along the coast; if the Vikings were sailing west, we would see them.

In the distance, through the orange and gold glow of the setting sun, we saw them. As we rode hard down the coast road, we couldn't take our eyes from the ships, their lights getting stronger – getting closer. I should have ridden for Winchester there and then, as Godric urged me to, but I was entranced by what I was peering at through the gaps of the trees.

The ships glided majestically along the River Hamble, their oars in rhythm like eagles' wings. At the front of each boat, animated by the torches beside them, glowed a golden beast head, biting the air, smoke snorting from its nostrils. Behind them hung huge yellow sails, rippling gently on the summer breeze, a black raven painted in their centre, seemingly flying towards us. Hanging over both sides of each boat, was a line of shields, the flickering light of the torches occasionally revealing their yellow stripes. It was a sight I will never forget.

The ships raised their oars, like a flock of birds lifting their feet to land, as they glided into the shore, their shallow draughts scrapping upon the riverbed. "We must leave now," Godric urged.

I knew he was right, yet I found it almost impossible to pull my eyes from the brightly painted boats, many of which were now beached below us. It was only when the men began to jump from the ships, that I snapped out of my trance. Hearing their boots upon the shingle, we mounted our horses and rode for Winchester.

Word of the Viking invasion had reached the villages before us, but we urged those who remained to run for the hills and the forests. A few villagers had reached Winchester before us, pleading at the gates to be allowed sanctuary within the city walls, but only when we arrived did the guards on duty believe the Vikings were near.

"Light the beacon and ring the bells," I screamed, over the cries of the panicking villagers beside me.

The beacon was lit, and by the time the gates had been opened to grant us entrance, other beacons could be seen in the distance, glowing bright, high upon their hill.

As the beacons spread, so did panic within Winchester. People were screaming and running, grabbing their loved ones by the hand. It was a storm of confusion: people not knowing whether they should run from the city or seek protection behind its walls.

I ran to the palace, expecting to see the king, but it was Bishop Swithun who met me, propped up on either side by a monk. "Where is Aethelbehrt?" I screamed.

"The king is not here," the bishop said. "And neither are many of his thanes."

"He must have ridden out to meet the Vikings," I said. "Let's hope he can talk them out of fighting."

"I doubt that," the bishop said, looking beyond me.

What I saw, when I turned around, ripped my heart from my chest. The Vikings' path towards us, burnt bright;

the villages we had ridden through ablaze, huge, thick smoke spiralling high, blacker than the night sky.

"There is no time to run Alfred…you must protect Wessex's treasure behind the walls of the minster," the bishop urged. "Along with the people who remain."

I nodded at perhaps the only person I trusted and shouted at the nearest guards for assistance. Most I told to bring the people behind the city walls, but I told the strongest looking three to help move the royal treasures from the palace chapel into the minster.

"The gold has gone Alfred, Aethelbehrt took it with him," the bishop said.

"So how can I protect Wessex's treasure, if it has already gone?" I shouted.

The bishop's smile surprised me: "Wessex's treasure hasn't gone…I'm talking to him. Nothing…nobody is more precious than you."

Godric and a Cornish guard lifted the bishop into the saddle, and they rode to the minster, shouting at all who would listen to follow them. I rode behind them, looking back at the balls of fire and smoke which were rolling ever nearer.

People streamed through the narrow gate within the walls, running past crates and barrels into the minster. I stood by the gate and shouted at my people who were silhouetted by the sky which burnt bright behind them. I helped an elderly couple through the gate, and once they had passed, Godric and I bolted the wooden gate shut. The thin gate, set within the walls, wouldn't hold the Vikings back, but it would slow them down.

Frantic conversations filled the minster. "Why bring us here?" I heard one man say, "this is exactly where the Vikings will think the treasure is buried."

Many muttered their agreement and I silently added mine.

Bishop Swithun shouted instructions to some of the guards, who ran back outside. Inside, people huddled together, their quiet, nervous chatter echoing around the minster. I walked with them, trying to reassure them, trying to look and sound more confident than I was. Nervous chatter turned to frantic cries, when the Vikings were heard marching into the city, the thumps of their axes upon their shields, striking terror into my people. My fascination got the better of me, and I opened a pair of shutters to look out upon my city. A long line of guards – men of Wessex and men of Cornwall – stood outside the minster, a flaming torch in one hand and a shield in the other, between us and the Danes who were marching, untroubled, into the city.

Like moths attracted to a flame, the Vikings swarmed towards us. They began to hack at the gates, each blow met with screams behind me. I looked at the people and they looked back at me, their eyes and faces wiped of hope. A bow and quiver of arrows lay at the feet of an elderly man, who was busy comforting his wife and children. I snatched them and rushed outside, brushing past the bishop and Godric, as they tried to call me back.

The Vikings stood where the gate once was. I strung my first arrow and aimed towards them, then four of my guards formed a protective shield wall around me. As the first Danes began to squeeze through the narrow gap in the wall, I loosed my arrow. It rattled into the stone wall. I strung and fired again, and again, this time my arrows thudded, as they found flesh. Vikings screamed and fell where I shot them, temporarily blocking their entrance. More men came. More men fell until all my arrows were spent. I had no idea how we could stop the Viking advance now, but my guards did.

One of them shouted at me to return to the minster, and with no arrows left, I did. I watched from my window as the guards lifted their shields and advanced towards the Vikings, their torches ablaze. Each guard threw their torch to the ground, and the earth burst into flames. The men ran back towards us, crouched behind their shields as they moved. Arrows rained down from the sky, most finding shields or earth, but some striking guards, their anguished screams piercing the night sky.

Those that had survived fell into the minster. A voice screamed from beyond the wall of fire. He was screaming my name: "Alfred…surrender yourself. We want you…not your people."

"That must be Weland," the bishop growled. "He cannot be trusted. He will kill you…then he will kill us all."

I didn't answer. A long line of shadows stood beyond the fire, the smoke hiding their faces but not their intentions, their axes and swords twitching with the flames.

Weland shouted again: "We offer a hostage exchange."

Bishop Swithun looked at me. "Who could he have as important as you?"

A shout answered his question: "Do not exchange yourself for me. Stay where you are Alfred."

Judith… The Vikings had her.

At once, I made for the door, but the guards pulled me back. "You must let me go," I urged the bishop, trying to loosen the guards' grip on my arm. I cannot let Judith die for me."

"Alfred…your duty is to your people. Without you, they have no hope. You will not sacrifice yourself." I had never heard the bishop speak so firmly.

Weland screamed again: "My men are fetching water

Alfred. These flames will soon die, and when they do, so will you and your people. Judith will be the first."

I stared out of the window, not knowing what to do. Weland was right: we were trapped, the fire wouldn't hold them back much longer. It was then that I felt a hand on my shoulder, I turned around and could barely believe the face within the hood.

"Hello Alfred," Mother whispered.

"But…what…how did you get into the minster?" I stammered.

"The same way that you're going to get out," she said.

It was only then that I realised that most of the people inside the minster had disappeared.

"There is a passage that leads from the crypt out into the woods beyond the city," Mother explained. "You need to go now Alfred."

Through the window, I could see a long line of Vikings, passing buckets of water along it towards the fire. "You must go now Alfred," the bishop urged.

"We must all go," I said, urging all who were left to follow the hooded woman.

The remaining guards began to barricade the door, dragging benches and tables to slow the Vikings' entrance. Godric and I propped the bishop's arms on our shoulders, and we followed my mother into the crypt and through the tunnels. Danish roars reached us, echoing down the tunnels, announcing their arrival at the minster's door.

We emerged from the tunnel, in the woods beyond the city and waited for the guards to emerge. They never did.

"If they had run for the tunnels, the Vikings would have followed," Mother explained. "They were brave men. We need to move from here or they will have died for nothing."

From the woods, high upon the hill, I looked down

on Winchester. With many of the buildings ablaze, it resembled the fires of hell. My mother put her hand on my arm: "The city can be built again," she said softly, "and you must survive to be the one to build it."

I took one long last look at the city, wondering just how many of our people had died tonight. Was Judith dead? Or was she too precious a prisoner to kill? It seems that the Vikings want me, and they will keep fighting and burning until they have me. In the days to come, the fate of Wessex, perhaps of the whole land, will be decided. Perhaps these will be the last words Godric writes in my diary, perhaps this is where my story ends...

June 4th

I spent the night huddled beside Mother, high upon the wooded hill. The night was almost as light as day: the bright, amber glow of the burning city lit up its walls. The lights from the city and the sounds of young children, whimpering in the woods, made it impossible to sleep.

When I walked amongst the people, they looked to me, and not to the old lady beside me. Children spoke to their mothers, as I spoke to mine; I was as afraid as they were, but I knew I couldn't show it. There was no king, but there was a prince, and they needed to take strength from him. I spoke to mothers and children and shook the hands of the elderly men who stood in a protective ring around us. I was talking to a farmer, who had swapped his sickle for a sword, when Bishop Swithun found me.

"We need to talk about our next move," the bishop said, beckoning me away from listening ears.

I had been thinking about this all night and had discussed the many options with my mother. Attacking the Vikings and rescuing Judith was what I wanted, but mother made me see sense. Godric nodded in agreement: he reminded me that there were many Viking ships moored close by, no doubt with little men to guard them, and that we could set sail away from danger. He said it would be ironic if we escaped from the Vikings on their boats. The thought amused me, and for a moment I considered it, but I wouldn't be going anywhere without Judith.

"You are far more important to Wessex than she is," Mother said. "You mustn't risk your life for hers."

Mother had every reason to dislike Judith, but Bishop Swithun's attitude surprised me: "I wouldn't worry about her," he said coldly. "She has survived this long without us – I think she will outlive us all."

Mother noticed my anguish: "And how would you rescue her Alfred? Look around you. Do you have the men to fight?"

A laugh came from behind me. "Why do they need to be men?" a familiar voice asked.

A small hooded figure, stood in front of a dozen more, held a sword in one hand and slowly revealed her face with the other. Mildryd smiled, as did the monks behind her, all of whom carried smiles and weapons.

"Looks like you could do with some help," Magen laughed, patting the elderly lookout on the shoulder, who bashfully wiped the sleep from his eyes.

"What's the plan Alfred?" Mildryd snarled. "When do I get to kill some Vikings?"

"Not today Mildryd," the bishop replied, much to her disproval. "We don't fight until we can win. The Vikings have many more men and weapons, at least for now, but we have something they don't, and we can use it to our advantage," he said, looking along a row of blank faces. He smiled at our confusion: "The answer is all around us," he added, with a soft smile.

I looked first at the people and then beyond them. I knew then what he meant. We didn't have the warriors or the weapons, but we did have something that could help us – I'm just not sure if it will be enough.

June 5th

We walked through the night beneath the cover of the forest with the smouldering city at our backs. Women carried children and men carried weapons, leaving behind their homes and the Vikings who had torched them.

"We shouldn't be walking away from them, we should be running towards them," Mildryd growled. "I haven't been spending months training these monks to run away."

Magen nodded his agreement, and the other monks nodded theirs. The monks seem keen to fight, I fear they may soon get their wish, and only then will we see how good a job Mildyrd has done.

As the skies lightened the trees parted to reveal a small settlement of round, wooden houses, surrounded by wooden fencing, each raised upon stilts. The houses could only be reached by scaling a steep grassy bank or by crossing a narrow wooden bridge. We chose the bridge, and as we walked over it, the children looked down at the geese and pigs who mingled together in the muddy marshland.

"And this is where we make our stand?" Mildryd scoffed.

"This is where we sleep," I replied. "That is where we fight."

All who were listening followed my finger towards the high hill beyond the village, the peak of which began to glow as the sun rose behind it. I lead my people over the bridge beneath the reddening sky, their nervous chatter and whispered conversations loud enough to wake some of the villagers, who wandered sleepily from their homes. None recognised me, but the moment they saw the bishop lower his hood, their fear fell from their faces.

The villagers made us all very welcome, providing us with food, warmth and beds. But as I sipped wine from my cup, I couldn't help feeling guilty. The villagers thought that we were here to protect them, but our very presence has put them in terrible danger.

"We had no choice," the bishop whispered, sensing my concern. "They have a better chance with us, than without us."

I looked at the small band of monks and elderly men who will stand between the Vikings and the villagers. "How can our men defeat the Vikings?" I muttered to the bishop.

"More men will come Alfred," the bishop replied, with far more confidence than I had.

"Do you think Jarl Sigurd will come?" I asked.

"He will come," the bishop said. "The question is, will he be fighting for us or against us?"

June 7th

Bishop Swithun was right: my family tree does have twisted branches; branches that look fine on the outside but are rotten within. Today I found out who the rotten branch is.

Mildryd shook me awake and I staggered from my bed, out into the weak morning sunshine. I looked to where she pointed: a lone horseman, high upon the hill, shimmered brightly in the morning haze. A small band of footmen stood on either side of the rider. Magen and the monks strung their bows, as the horseman trotted closer. He took a few steps more before I recognised the rider.

"Magen! Tell your monks to lower their weapons," I called, loud enough for the mounted man on the hill to hear.

Magen paused for a moment, looking first to the hill and then back to me, before instructing his men to lower their weapons. He, however, held his sword aloft. "He didn't tell me to lower my sword, did he?" Magen snarled, to the monk beside him.

"AETHELRED!" I shouted in surprise. "It's good to see you!"

I looked to the hill behind him, expecting Jarl Sigurd and his Viking warriors to follow. There was still no sign of them when Aethelred dismounted. He hugged me tight, but noticed, when he released me, that my eyes were on the hill.

"Sigurd said that he will follow soon," Aethelred explained, with little belief in his voice. "He said that there were things he had to take care of first."

Bishop Swithun had hobbled over in time to hear this. Supported by a monk either side, he smiled weakly. Our numbers had been bolstered by thirteen men and one horse – hardly enough to turn the fight in our favour.

That night, I heard – and saw – just what we were up against. The drums came first: a light tap, like rain on a roof, became a pounding thud, shaking the ground and scattering the birds from the woods. We looked from the bridge, as flames bobbed through the trees, glowing brighter. Then the drums fell silent and the flames stopped moving, forming a wall of fire on the edge of the forest.

"We must act now Alfred, before it's too late," the bishop

warned. "You know what needs to be done."

I nodded and said my farewell to my mother. She hugged me tight and for longer than she had ever done before. "Your brother – the king – should be doing this," she whispered, wiping a tear from her eye.

Aethelred and his dozen warriors walked behind me over the long wooden bridge that stretched out into the night, towards the forest. Seeing our approach, the torches between the trees began to shake, dancing to the rhythm of the Viking drums. Three figures on horseback, each holding a flame low in one hand, slowly emerged from the trees, silhouetted by the torches behind them and accompanied by a frenzied, deafening drumbeat. We quickened our pace to meet them, wanting to keep them to the forest's edge. The figure in the middle waved his flame and the drums stopped.

"Halt!" shouted a voice, bone-chillingly familiar.

Weland held a torch, the light revealing his scared skull and hollowed cheeks.

Ignoring his command, we quickened our pace. As we advanced towards the Vikings, my heartbeat kept pace with my feet. Weland steadied his horse, as did the warriors on either side of him. They pulled out their axes, torchlight catching their sharpened edges.

I pulled my sword from my scabbard and thrust it into the ground. My brother, and his men, did the same, and we stood, behind a low wall of iron, only a spear's length away from the Vikings.

Weland threw his axe and it landed at my feet. His men laughed. Mine shook in fear. Trying to hide my fear, I pulled the axe slowly from the ground and returned it to the outstretched hand.

"You won't need that tonight Weland," I said, fighting

my nerves. “Not if you surrender.”

Weland’s laughed and his men laughed too when he translated my words.

“Why would we surrender to farmers and monks, to women and children?” the Viking sneered.

I hesitated for a moment and the Viking pounced upon it.

“That’s right Alfred…we have been watching you. Do you think I haven’t seen your…army?”

He laughed again, louder and for longer, the chainmail beneath his coned helmet rattling. His warriors joined in and they laughed together.

“You haven’t seen everything,” Aethelred interrupted. “A huge army of Saxon and Viking warriors are camped beyond the hill.”

“Vikings? Do you mean Sigurd’s men?” Weland chuckled.

I could sense Aethelred’s nervous eyes on me. “And the king’s army is close by,” I bluffed, desperately trying to sound convincing.

“Then I should kill you now!” Weland roared.

“Kill me, and you’ll never have peace or Wessex!” I replied. “You’ll be hunted down and killed, either by Saxon sword or Viking axes. Leave now and we will allow you safe passage back to your boats. You can keep your plunder.”

Weland sat still and silent for a moment, before he spoke to his men in their tongue.

“You will have your answer at daybreak,” Weland said calmly.

I nodded my approval, but my relief lasted just a moment. The shadow of another horse emerged from the wood, two figures on its back, the one at the front much the smaller. I recognised Queen Judith’s frightened cry long before I could see her face.

"If you attack, she will be the first to die. Then it will be you Alfred," Weland sneered. He rode beside Judith and held his torch to her face. She looked at me through terrified eyes, a knife to her throat. Before she could speak, the Viking turned the horse on its hooves, and it galloped back to the torch-lit woods, with Weland and his men following behind.

Bishop Swithun and Mother showed little emotion when I told them what had happened. They felt no pity towards Judith, but I did, and that's why I decided to return to the Viking camp and free her. The only person I told was Mildryd, because she was the only person coming with me.

Mildryd and I had discussed the plan privately: creep into the forest, find Judith, distract the men guarding her, cut her free of her ropes, and flee into the forest to meet back at the village. We did find Judith, but we didn't need to distract the guards or cut her free because she was neither guarded nor bound.

We heard her before we could see her: her laugh lighter and higher than the raucous bellowing around her. When we crept closer, we could see her, through the gaps in the trees. She was sat around a blazing fire, laughing with the Vikings – a cup in one hand and a hawk on the other. My hawk – Hilda. Mildryd could see the shock in my eyes. What I heard next ripped my insides out.

The laughter fell and Judith began to speak, in French, hiding her words from all except Weland and me. I strained my ears to hear them, barely believing the words she spoke. Mildryd didn't need to speak French to understand – she could see it on my ashen face.

The rustle of leaves behind me broke my trance. Before I could turn, a huge hand grabbed my face and muffled my mouth. Its fingers grabbed my jaw and twisted my head towards his. I looked first at the Viking helmet and then to the wide, wild, white eyes below.

"He said you'd be here," Jarl Sigurd whispered, grabbing me by the hand.

For a moment, I thought he was about to drag me towards the feasting Danes; it was a great relief to be out of the woods, heading back to the village.

I gathered everyone together: Mildryd, Mother, Bishop Swithun, Jarl Sigurd and Aethelred sat on benches, as I explained what Judith had said.

I was amazed that neither Mother nor the bishop seemed surprised. It was an outraged Aethelred who spoke first: "Why does she want the Vikings to attack us? Why does she want us dead Alfred?"

"She wants Wessex. She has always wanted Wessex," Mother's voice was cold and hard, "and she can't have it whilst my boys still breathe."

The bishop noticed the realisation on my face. "That's right Alfred. It was Judith who tried to kill you and Aethelred. In the river, on your horses and in your beds. Her men. She wrote the letter, bringing you back to Winchester. I thought she and Aethelbald wanted you dead…but your brother had nothing to do with it. He was trying to keep you safe."

I didn't think. I didn't breathe. I just shouted the words: "Why didn't you tell me?"

The bishop, helped by Jarl Sigurd, staggered weakly to his feet, and I instantly regretted my outburst. "I wasn't sure until today. And you had to see her treachery to believe it."

"You knew I'd try and free her," I asked, contritely.

The bishop nodded. "Yes…I thought you would. Your heart is bigger than your head Alfred."

"Time for talking is over," Jarl Sigurd roared. "It's time to fight."

June 10th

What happened here, these last two days, needs to be remembered forever. Those who fought, especially those that fell, must never be forgotten. Their deeds will be immortalised in words and song. Poets will sing, in every corner of the kingdom, heralding the bravery of those whose sacrifice saved Wessex…

The Viking's answer came, as they emerged from the woods in the half-light, their shields locked together in row after row. I watched from the village, Aethelred and Mildryd beside me, as the black and yellow striped shields moved through the mist, like an army of angry bees. They stopped and signalled their intent, shaking the heavens by thumping their swords and axes against their shields.

We then signalled our intent. Magen, the monks and the elderly men from Wessex, raised themselves above the wooden fencing and let loose their arrows. Some fell short but many more thudded into the Viking's wooden shield wall, screams of pain rose from behind the splintered shields. However, the Viking lines remained together – any gaps were quickly filled by locking shields. The men fired again, with Mildryd joining them, but their efforts and arrows did little to stop the slow advance of the Vikings. As they neared the long bridge, the Viking lines wheeled, forming a long, black and yellow snake that began to slither through the marshland towards us.

"Now!" I screamed.

The archers lifted their arrows which dripped with oil, and as Mildryd ran along them with her torch, each burst into flame. Streaks of light pierced the mist as the blazing arrows flew down towards the Vikings. The Vikings, however, were not the target, the bridge was, with the arrows thumping into the carpet of oily hay that covered it. The bridge burst into a thin road of fire, confusing the enemy.

Some charged the bridge but they only made a few steps before they threw themselves, blazing and burning, into the waters below. Most turned from the bridge and made for the steep banks, many floundering or falling into the marshy ground. Arrows continued to rain down upon the Vikings, those stuck in the marshland soon lay sinking into watery graves.

With our arrows spent, the steep banks begin to fill with Vikings. On my command, the men and Mildryd behind the fence, lifted the long logs and sent them rolling towards their target. Shouts and screams filled the air, and men fell back down to the foot of the hills, some not to rise again.

The Vikings were down, but they would come again, and we had little to stop them. Aethelred jumped upon a horse, pulled me up with his free hand, and together we rode from the village, towards the hill with Mildryd and the monks at our tail. We stopped near the top of the hill and looked down upon the Vikings, who had now reformed their long lines of linked shields and were making their way towards us, moving around the edge of the village.

"There must be five hundred, perhaps even six hundred of the devils," Aethelred said nervously.

"All the more to kill then," Mildryd snarled.

As they neared the foot of the hill, the Viking lines closed, each warrior overlapping his shield with the one beside. They advanced together, forming a wedge as they went. Weland strode onwards with his largest, fiercest fighters beside him, brandishing their weapons and screaming at us. Then we heard another huge scream: not from the Vikings below us but from the Vikings above us. They charged past, their shields overlapping, with Jarl Sigurd at the head of the wedge, trading obscenities with Weland's men. With their swords raised, both armies advanced, like two iron arrowheads about to collide. Collide they did with such ferocity that they lifted the clouds and split the sky. With the advantage of the hill, Sigurd and his warriors thundered into Weland's wedge, punching a hole at the sides with their swinging swords and axes. Weapons found wood and weapons found flesh, warriors screamed, lying on the hill, as a red river washed over them. Sigurd's charge ended, stopped by the falling bodies at their feet and the sea of men before them. Weland rallied his forces and they began to push their Viking brothers and sisters back up the hill. I ran down the hill, as did Mildryd and the monks, and together we joined Sigurd's army, as we tried to resist the advance.

A Viking shield pushed hard against mine. My arms and legs stretched in agony as they failed to hold back my opponent. I felt my legs buckle beneath me and I fell back, looking up to see a pair of wild white eyes and an axe swinging for me. Another axe swung, this time to my side, and clattered into the one ahead of me. A foot kicked against the shield in front of me, knocking it back. Jarl Sigurd pulled me up to my feet.

"You should stick to playing Tafl Alfred," he roared.

Back on my feet, I braced myself, as I tried to push back against the steel wave. To my left, Mildryd was holding her ground, pushing her shield hard with the one hand, and slashing her sword with the other. The ground shook as one line of Weland's men crashed into another, and another, their combined strength sending many of our fighters to the ground. Some were pulled up but many more disappeared beneath the iron-shod boots of the throng.

The push against us became a surge, our lines breaking and retreating, back towards the top of the hill. If they pushed us back to the top the fight would be lost, as would Wessex.

Weland's men stepped over the fallen, and formed a circle of death around us, each of his men brandishing a weapon, some holding two. Slowly they advanced towards us, closing the noose around us.

"Behind me," Sigurd screamed, holding his shield over me and Mildryd. "On me."

Some of the largest, most blood-splattered men joined him. The sky blackened as they formed a shield wall above me, and slowly they began to walk forward.

"Get ready Alfred, we've going to try and punch a hole," Sigurd yelled.

I found a gap in the shields and peered through it. Weland's wall was so thick with men, I couldn't see how we could break it. Beyond his wall, I could see Judith, dressed in a bright red cloak with a crown upon her head and Hilda my hawk on her hand.

"Ready Alfred?" Sigurd asked.

I gripped my sword in one hand and held Mildryd with the other. "It's been my honour to fight beside you Alfred," she said, without a flicker of emotion.

Our shields pressed hard against each other, as we readied ourselves for the charge. I thought first of Mother, and then of the bishop, hoping they were far away, out of danger.

Jarl Sigurd turned his shield and spoke to me, allowing me one last look at Wessex.

"Wait!" I shouted. "Wait!"

"Don't be afraid Alfred. We win or we die a decent death with swords in our hands," Sigurd said.

"Look!" I said.

When he looked, Sigurd lowered his shield, as did the warriors around him. Weland's men were no longer advancing in a circle, they were running for their lives. They too had seen the thousands of men, spilling from the woods to the north, riding hard beneath the banners of Wessex and Cornwall. As they galloped closer, roared on by cheers from the hill, I saw Osric at the head of the army, his sons Wulfstan and Wulfric and Bishop Eahlstan beside him, leading the charge towards the Vikings, who were now fleeing back to their boats.

Heavy legged but light-headed, I ran down the hill, Mildryd and Sigurd beside me. I stood facing the galloping army, the ground trembling beneath their hooves, praying that I would be recognised.

"Stop!" I screamed, waving my arms frantically.

They didn't stop, if anything, they quickened their gallop. I shouted again, and again, as the ocean of horses came closer, spray from their hooves carried on the summer's breeze. "STOP!"

Osric was the first to pull his horse up and then each man in turn followed. He dismounted, his horse held by Wulfstan, and waded through the marshland towards us.

"Alfred!" he said, clasping my arm in his. "It's good to see you."

He looked to the ground beneath him and before him. "Thank you, Alfred," he said. "We would have sunk into this marsh if you hadn't warned us to halt."

"The heathens are escaping," Bishop Eahlstan shouted, his white robes gathering mud as he walked.

"Let them run," I said. "Let them tell everyone what they faced today."

"That would be the king's decision Alfred," Osric smiled weakly, "And we will have to wait some time for that."

June 18th

A week of feasting has finally finished – who would have thought drinking, eating and cheering could be so exhausting. Much to my embarrassment, the biggest cheers were for me, no doubt because of the rousing, drunken speeches that Jarl Sigurd has been giving. With Vikings prepared to fight alongside Saxons, Wessex seems to be stronger than ever, but the same can't be said for the king. Aethelbehrt can throw all the feasts and celebrations he wants, but the people, myself included, will never forget that he fled his people when they most needed him. He may be able to rebuild Winchester but I'm not sure he will ever be able to rebuild his reputation. His grip on the throne is much looser, loose enough Jarl Sigurd believes for me to snatch it from him, but there has been enough bloodshed and treachery. It's time for this family to grow strong roots. Aethelred too, has had praise heaped upon him, for he fought bravely, and did our people proud. But now, in this fragile peace, he has put down the sword once again and picked up the bible. He can read it to himself now. Learning my letters is also my priority, and on our return to Winchester, I will talk to Bishop Swithun about it. Godric, more than any other, is desperate for me to learn so that I can write my own diary.

"It was bad enough hearing the fighting," Godric the Unsteady muttered, "then you made me write about it."

Mother didn't come with us to Shelbourne. Only a few people know that she lives, and she wants to keep it this way.

July 25th

Bishop Swithun has done a tremendous job overseeing the repairs at Winchester. The first thing he did was make sure that there were new homes for the people to move into. When they were housed, the people then showed their thanks by helping rebuild the walls and the palace.

The king led us through the gate to polite applause, but when Mildryd, Aethelred and I trotted into the city, the throngs of people, lining the streets, erupted with rapturous cheers. I climbed from my horse and shook the hands that had helped rebuild the city. Each of them smiled, but no smile was wider than the one Bishop Swithun wore.

I walked to him and helped him into his seat. His hand was cold and weak as I held it, but the words he said were strong. "Look at the people. Your people. They love you Alfred. One day soon you will rule them, and I know that you will be a great king. Alfred the Great – that is how you will be remembered."

Also in this series...

ISBN: 9781906132521

UK: £7.99

Dishonest, cunning and cruel, King John was so bad that even his mother despised him! Fighting his brothers for the crown, he stabbed them in the back at every opportunity. Where did it all go wrong for this notorious ruler? Find out in this revealing royal diary.

By the same author

Paul Nolan has a passion for historical fiction. His first book *Demons of Dunkirk* was published in 2015.

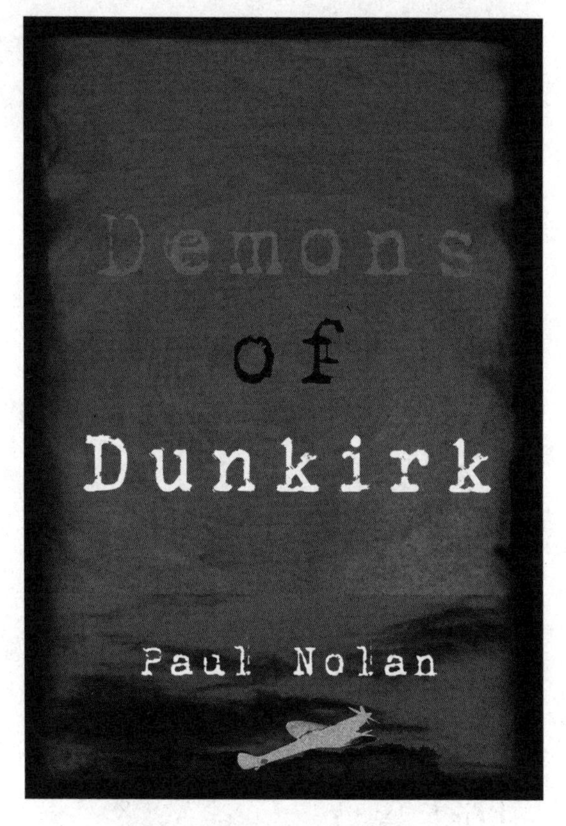

ISBN: 9781906132477

UK: £7.99

‘This is an unputdownable adventure story woven around the evacuation at Dunkirk and then the D-Day landings but from a different angle... Packed with historical facts but written as fiction this is a thrilling read.” *Lovereading.co.uk*

http://www.mogzilla.co.uk/demonsofdunkirk

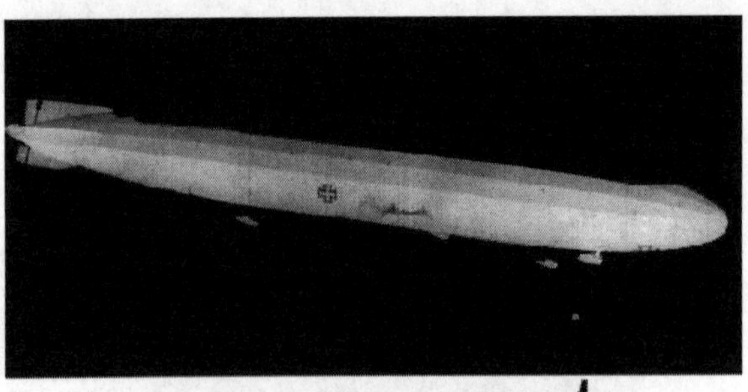

agent two face

PAUL NOLAN

Agent Two Face

ISBN:9781906132408

£7.99

Reading age: 9-14 years

Captured by spymasters, a German teenager soon finds himself living a secret life within wartime London. Danger lurks everywhere, as he awaits his mission. When it comes, he discovers his very success could win the Great War for Germany. His mission takes him from the bombed streets of London to the horrors of the Western Front.

The Age of Bronze

ISBN: 9781906132460

£7.99

Reading age: 6-10 years

A boy and a girl wake up within a stone circle. Before they can return home to their own time, they have to steal an artefact from the vicious Beaker Tribe and restore the stone circle to its former glory. Will they succeed? Or will they be cast in bronze forever?

WAR
STORY